WAR SERVICE

Eilleen Gardner Galer

AUTHOR:	Eilleen Gardner Galer
DESIGNERS:	Anne Pace
	Lou Chap
COVER ILLUSTRATION:	Anne Pace
PUBLISHER & EDITOR:	H. Donald Kroitzsh
ASSISTANT EDITORS:	Barbara Ritchotte
	Anne Pace

Printed in Canada

Published by:
Five Corners Publications, Ltd.
HCR 70, Box 2
Plymouth, Vermont 05056—USA

War Service
ISBN: 1-886699-05-4

War Hero

The miserable pup by the side of the road
Abandoned - his folks sped away.
Whimpering and scared, as traffic whizzed by
Dare he budge, this would be his last day.

Thus, cruelly, began the epic tale
Of a noble and courageous dog.
In wartime to come, he would save men's lives
His missions so brave filled the log.

He served in the South Pacific,
As messenger from front lines to back.
Through Hell he pursued his perilous way
To warn of impending attack.

He must pass through a curtain of gunfire,
Swim a river that seemed miles wide,
Jump a barbed wire fence of protection,
And find his handler inside.

The day he was shot he still struggled on.
This soldier was no prima donna.
No less than the men whose lives he saved,
He merited a Medal of Honor.

by Eilleen Gardner Galer

WAR SERVICE

∾

Chapter I

Young Jay Malone had nobody but himself to blame for his misfortune. Which made it all the harder to bear. One stupid kid trick changed his whole life. If only he hadn't teased a tacky little old girl he detested, his glory dreams of a military career might not have ended before he was fifteen.

It was Friday and the beginning of vacation. Elated that his report card was excellent, but unhappy with the prospect of summertime parting from his friends, he stayed after school for one last ball game. And his side won. Feeling good, his tattered cap on the back of his head and a cocky smile on his peaked little face, he set out briskly for the long walk home.

Turning a corner he overtook the youngest Willey dawdling along a quiet stretch between the Episcopal Churchyard and the jailhouse (unoccupied at the time). She was a skinny figure in saggy, wash-faded pink dress and crooked run-over shoes. Below taffy colored pigtails her big ears stood out. For Jay the provocation was irresistible.

"Donkey ears!" he taunted.

She looked back, wrinkled up her little pug nose and stuck our her tongue. Oh, what an ugly face!

"Donkey ears!"

She picked up a big oyster shell not yet crushed in the street paving and sailed it at him with all her might.

He let out a bloodcurdling yell, his hand covering one eye.

With a look of horror the littlest Willey turned and fled.

The strike left Jay half blinded. But instinct for self-preservation spurred him to frantic flight also. Terrified lest someone happened to be watching, he dodged through the church gateway, ran across the cemetery as fast as his spindling legs could carry him, and through side streets empty of people doubled back to the train depot at the edge of town where he arrived breathless, his heart pounding. Full of woe, he began his walk out to the farm. He had two and a half miles to go.

Torn between fear and fury, his head throbbing, he trudged miserably out the long straight stretch of road that seemed endless, thankful not to meet anyone. And he kept wishing, futilely, that he could go back and begin the day over. If only he had gone straight home. Or the ball game had lasted just five minutes longer. If only he had sense enough to keep his big mouth shut! Somebody ought to give him a good swift kick. He stumbled along, cursing like a man but crying like a baby.

Still, the damage had been done. And he could only brood over it. Sure knowledge of the girl's fright gave him a wry satisfaction. If anybody should ask, he was willing to bet that she'd live in terror for days to come, expecting to be arrested and led off to jail. Little stupid!

Click of the gate latch as he entered their short lane brought his Golden Retriever bounding joyfully to greet him. Usually he gave Josh loving small talk and a good wooling about the ears. But now he only hugged him tight, and his tears fell on the top of the big dog's head. After a bit, he wiped his good eye on his sleeve and apprehensively went on to the house.

Relieved to find his mother out some place, he took a look in the mirror and winced. Wetting one edge of the roller towel, he dabbled cold water onto the bruise. Then buttering a leftover biscuit for himself and one for Josh, he took his pal out to sit on the porch steps. The devoted dog pressed close, trying dumbly to comfort him.

There his mother found the disconsolate pair and hustled Jay into the house for a bread poultice of stale crumbs soaked in vinegar.

"You're late getting home," she softly scolded. "And now this."

"I stayed awhile for our last ball game," he mumbled.

Fussing over him, she said no more. And since she seemed to blame rough play for his accident, he didn't intend to change her mind.

Never afterward could he bring himself to breathe the truth to a soul. But secretly a heavy burden of worry weighed upon his mind, for his vision was impaired. As he learned to live with it, he found some comfort that his injury seemed not very noticeable to others. The light gray of his eyes camouflaged the milky scar that blurred his sight. And he always tried to act natural, just as before, never letting on that he was not as sharp as the next fellow. It was his determination to appear normal that brought about his second, near-fatal accident.

Helping to haul in hay by moonlight, he misjudged his footing on top of the load and took a hard fall. It startled the horses and the wagon lurched. One hind wheel narrowly missed crushing Jay's head. But an outcropping of rock gave him a severe hip injury that left him lame.

Housebound, he silently fumed over his damned rotten luck. His mother, devoutly thankful that he had not been killed, was at a loss to understand his dark moodiness. Little did she dream the depths of his despair. One calamity after another had chalked off his life's dearest wish. From the time he was just a little sprout engrossed in complicated maneuvers with his toy armies he had wanted to be a soldier when he grew up. Now he was unfit. He would never be the third generation Malone to serve in the armed forces.

His grandfather Malone, the first John Jay, and a colorful veteran of the Civil War, had fired the boy's imagination.

His father, John Jay II, was even then with the U. S. fighting forces in France.

And he, John Jay III, had confidently expected to follow in their footsteps. Some day he too would bravely serve his country.

Now all was lost. He hadn't a chance. And he wondered glumly what a fellow like him had to live for. Pampering his hip in a cushioned chair on the porch, with Josh to keep him company, and not much else to do but fret, his thoughts by turns angry or despairing, he scowled at the sultry landscape. Its emptiness irritated him. The fields and the creek were lifeless under the noonday sun.

Then a bearded man in his boat chugged through the narrows and headed across wide water toward the long wooded point where tall pines, toppled by tidal erosion, lay strewn dead and dying along the shore. About the same time, their neighbor lady appeared in her buggy going to town. Her old horse rarely moved out of a walk, but she kept jerking the reins and slapping his bony rump with a little switch that still had a few green leaves on its tip end. She was a withered, hard-faced old person, and not particularly sociable with kids. Jay shifted his chair so as to be invisible.

Sight of these inoffensive folk only irritated him the more, for it was just the likes of them that peopled the whole locality. Kids were scarce. Any boys his age were too far away for easy comradeship.

It was so different from the old home town back in Pennsylvania where he lived contentedly amongst relatives and a nice lot of friends. Here there could be no bursting out the front door and running across the street or up the

3

block with some marvelous secret or hot new idea. And bright ideas, if not immediately shared. had a way of fizzling.

His anger welled up afresh that after his Dad left for the front his mother had been persuaded to make the move down here to Maryland. He'd had to leave behind all his buddies. Here, the fellows he liked at school lived on farms too remote for spur of the moment camaraderie. He bemoaned his fate.

Josh laid his head in Jay's lap and gave him that long loving look. The boy's small brown hand with ragged fingernails reached to stroke the patient dog's head. But for Jay his summer just beginning would be unbearable. Besides the lonesomeness, his life had been ruined here. He hated the place.

Last year he'd had such glorious visions of himself. He'd felt so proud and so sure that it was just a matter of time until he became a soldier. Last year . . . Thinking back on the joy of it choked him up.

★ ★ ★

Chapter II

Decoration Day was at hand. As always on that occasion, Jay's beloved grandfather, Captain Malone, shone with full military luster. Wearing his Union Blue and carrying the flag, the old gentleman marched at the head of the parade to the cemetery.

Grampa rose earlier than usual and dressed with care. Then as folks were out setting flags or tacking bunting to the gingerbread of their fancy old porches, he took his dignified way down to the Square. There the band warmed up while the chosen members of all four churches settled upon their places in the parade line. It happened the same every year. No sooner had Grampa Malone passed by than Bill Garman appeared next door, hurrying importantly down his front steps with his instrument. The others had nickel horns, but Bill played a big brass tuba, which puffed him with pride. Mrs. Garman, equally proud and out to see him off, would call over, "Are you going down to the Square, Mrs. Malone?"

And Jay's plump, pretty mother, carefully adjusting their flag, invariably replied, "No. We thought we'd go on out to the cemetery and be there for the services." She and his Dad liked to stand with the familiar crowd among the tombstones for the best view of the parade.

But Jay stayed where he could follow the pageant from beginning to end. This annual disinterment of uniforms and old weapons thrilled him. More so than Christmas, even.

For its size their town could muster a surprising number of veterans, fifty-two years after the close of the Civil War. There was also one crusty rebel, living up the valley with his Yankee son-in-law. But Mr. Morgan remained aloof and never paraded his Confederate Gray, although he had been invited. The others, however, were all on hand that fair morning. Down on the grassy Square by the bandstand, four old Union soldiers stood in the shade of the maples, idly waiting. They wore their uniforms—dark blue jackets with light blue trousers, and the little toptilted cap—all very neat, buttons and buckles bright, their black shoes polished to a high shine.

Their muskets too were tidy, the barrels and metal trim gleaming. To spare the old soldiers needless fatigue, their weapons would be carried by "younger oldsters" and later fired across the graves. There burned in Jay a secret resentment that he was considered too young to take part.

The veterans included Dad Seltzer, a jolly old chap with long beard snowy white and nearly down to his waist, who was always natty-looking and spry. And Pappy Heckert, heavy-featured and close-shaven, his right arm off below the elbow (it was amazing the strength he had in that stump), his sleeve pinned over. Mr. Bricker, the oldest and most withered, was a spare little man with droopy eyelids, thin pale mustache sagging down to his chin, and ill-fitting false teeth too big for his face; yet he was described as quite a lady-killer in his day.

Most martial was Captain Malone. Medium tall of person and very erect, he had deepset sharp dark eyes and snow-white beard neatly trimmed. Tiny crossed sabers decorated his cap; and the real weapon hung by his side. Jay admired him extravagantly. He could just see the Captain leading a cavalry charge, riding with sword held high. It was a little matter of pay, Grampa once confided, that caused him to join the cavalry. Cavalry privates received twelve dollars a month; the Infantry and Artillery had to make do with eleven.

Dad Seltzer was full of himself that morning. He executed a jig with his stiff old legs. Tapping Mr. Bricker on the shoulder, he piped up, "You're older'n I am, I bet. How old be ye?" cupping his ear with a shaky hand. "Eighty-one! I knowed it. Why, I'm only seventy-eight. I'm just a lad yet. At heart anyway. Heh, heh."

Pappy Heckert made some roguish response that was drowned out and gave a little left-handed salute.

Full of pranks then, soon the old boys would put on solemn faces befitting the occasion and take their places, ready to perform with dignity the tribute to their comrades who had passed on.

The band stopped blowing discordant toots and struck up a lively tune. The order of the parade having been settled, there was commotion and bustle as the march got underway. Jay, on the sidelines eagerly watching, chuckled at the comical column. Ahead, Grampa strode along with proud bearing. Next, Dad Seltzer took his short quick steps. Behind him the other two old soldiers rocked along: Pappy Heckert, wounded in the thigh, limped to the right. Mr. Bricker, with one leg shorter than the other, dipped to the left.

Next came the band, clothed in dark blue with gold braid, cheeks puffed, and Will Feaser beating the big drum carried by Indigo Ike who was not musical.

For some reason the procession halted. Grampa Malone, espying Jay, beckoned. And when once more the onward march began, the boy had a place between the veterans and the band. He carried a small silk flag. Proud? Oh, my, yes. But just a little bit wistful. If only he had his own uniform, a miniature of the oldsters', like the little drummer boy in his picture at home, with a tasseled red sash and an eagle painted on his drum.

To martial airs they marched along Main Street, up High, and out the valley road past the Ebersole farm. Thick hedgerows in places cut off any little breeze, and the sun beat down. But welcome shade lay under a row of old black cherry trees. The horns glinted sunlight and belched thunderous music. A flock of white pigeons alight on the Ebersole barn flew up in alarm and wheeled about. Two brown horses solemnly watched over the half-doors. The shoes of the marchers became coated with powdery dust. And Jay, feeling thirsty, longed for a drink from the good cold spring cupped under the hill below the cemetery. Conscious of the watching townspeople, he marched gravely, a little bit chesty, sure that the other kids were dying of envy.

Though he joined in lustily singing America to begin and The Star Spangled Banner that closed the program, his mind wandered during a reading of Lincoln's Gettysburg Address and the oration delivered by an out-of-town dignitary. He meanwhile feasted his eyes upon a pretty little girl he very much admired in his class at school. In stiffly starched white dress, her dark hair in curls, she stood clutching her mother's hand. Catching his glance, she smiled shyly and looked down at her strapped shoes. The band selections stirred everybody. But when the old muskets spoke and the bugle notes were sad, it was almost more than Jay could bear.

The faded flags replaced by bright new ones, with pretty garden flowers everywhere, folks began to mingle, telling each other how nice their graves looked.

★ ★ ★

~

Chapter III

The year was 1917. And already another conflict had begun. When on April 6th the US declared war on Germany, their whole town responded with patriotic fervor. A mass meeting was called, a holiday proclaimed. School was let out, the stores closed. In his excitement Jay nearly ran his legs off, trying to be everywhere, to see everything.

Reading their newspaper spread out on the kitchen floor, he had followed the war from the torpedoing of the Lusitania by a German submarine. Those big black headlines—three inches high across the whole front page—gave him the shivers. And after America got into it, the news was all about how the country had "demonstrated a patriotic enthusiasm never seen before".

Jay thrilled to the town's eagerness to throw itself into the war effort. Men wanted to fight the Huns. And impatient for the call to arms, they met down on the Square to drill of their own accord, while neighbors, including the old veterans, gathered to watch.

Boys big and little ran wild, destroying the enemy with their toy guns, yelling, "Pow! Pow! Pow!" Jay, waving his stick sword and screaming orders, led the peewee fighting forces pell-mell through the brush down along the canal in maneuvers of his own planning.

Before the first names were drawn in July under the Selective Service Act, some of the younger men, Jay's father among them, had enlisted. And the shrill voices of their offspring gathered in clusters could be heard boasting, "My Dad's going next week." Or, "Huh, mine's gone already!"

John Malone joked about it. Already thirty, he hadn't time to lose, he said, if he wanted to do his bit. Jay last saw his father boarding the midnight train. Standing tall, he solemnly promised Dad that he would look after Mom. And he meant to. But that seemed like dull business alongside soldiering. If only he were old enough.

Not long after, destiny intruded unpleasantly in their quiet affairs.

The morning being cool, Mrs. Malone got early to work canning tomatoes. And she sent Jay out, hoping to sell some of the head lettuces from their small "Victory" garden. He could get maybe ten or fifteen cents each for them.

Thinking they might hear from his Dad, Jay stopped by the Post Office. But their only mail was a letter from Uncle Joe, his mother's brother, who lived on a farm down in Maryland.

Mrs. Malone sank into her rocker and quickly slit the envelope with a hairpin. Jay pulled out a dining chair, sat down and laid his cap over his knee.

The letter told a tragic story. Uncle Joe had just lost his entire family. George, their grown son who worked in Philadelphia, had come home very sick and died three days later. Then Aunt Martha came down with it (he didn't say what) and she lasted only one week. Uncle Joe said he was managing. But he wondered if maybe they wouldn't like to come stay with him for the duration.

Mrs. Malone and Jay locked stares. That they should leave their comfortable niche in the old home town had not once occurred to either of them.

Jay shook his head and said with finality, "No!"

His mother nodded, agreeing. Yet troubling thoughts disturbed her. Joe was her only living relative. Just they two were left of the family. And he had always been good to her. The poor man doubtless found it terrible hard. She knew what loneliness was.

She spoke only of practical matters. "In a way," she said slowly, "it would be a big help to us for money. Not needing the house rent, we'd be able to save for when Dad comes home."

Jay kept shaking his head stubbornly.

"And the food bills. Uncle Joe wrote one time that their creek was full of fish and crabs for the taking."

Still Jay balked. But Mrs. Malone, against her will, could think of more reasons for going than not. In their present beggarly circumstances (even their modest contributions to the church collection plate had dwindled), they should be thankful for Uncle Joe's generous invitation.

To avoid argument, she said, "We'll have to sleep on it," and folded the letter into her apron pocket. "Perhaps you'd take that pan of peelings down on the lot for me?"

Carrying the heavy dishpan down the boardwalk to the pit they wanted filled up, Jay could see two of his buddies hanging around their fort in the weedlot by the canal. Sight of them fired up his anger at the thought of moving away. He got so mad that when he went to heave in his load, he heaved himself in with it. Sputtering, he crawled out plastered with tomato skins.

His mother standing with her hands on her hips at the screen door saw him and laughed. Venting his fury would take some of the steam out of his resistance to leaving. All she said to him was, "Those loose boards have got to be fixed."

Over the weekend while they "slept on it," she enlisted the aid of Grampa Malone. After church he came home with them for Sunday dinner. They would have everybody's favorite dessert, kasha kuchen—cherry cake. And to salve up Jay, she made his favorite treat, what he called "slop pie." It was simply the pastry trimmings rolled into a crust, covered with milk, and sprinkled with sugar and spices. Jay was fond of it for snacking.

While she was busy washing up, Grampa and Jay had the back porch to themselves. Seeming without guile, the old gentleman said, "I brung you a book I think you'll like. It's cram full of facts and stories about the old war." He handed over a rather dog-eared volume in dark blue covers stamped in gold letters Blue and Gray.

With a little smile Jay politely accepted the relic, studying its cover. Sunk into the fabric were two flags, and in a gold circle two soldiers stood shaking hands. It was thick, more than eight hundred pages, he saw, leafing through.

Grampa added, "Until school begins and you get acquainted down there, you'll have time for reading, I should think."

A shadow passed over Jay's face, but he did not voice his discontent.

Grampa gave him a sharp glance, fingering his beard. "I know you hate to go away. But so did your Dad. Still, he figgered it was his duty. And helping out your Uncle Joe is kinda the same for you and your Ma."

Jay screwed up his face and shrugged. He was not in the habit of arguing with his Grampa.

"Think of all the adventures you'll have. I shouldn't wonder but what you'd learn to ride a horse good as any cavalryman—"

"There ain't no justice," Jay muttered, hardly to the point, but the kids thought the expression so clever.

"Well, mebbe not," Grampa quietly agreed. "But we all have to make sacrifices sometime or other. And fer a young feller, spending time on a farm seems like an easy way to do your part."

Still, Jay was unhappy at the prospect. "We'll be way off in the middle of nowhere," he whispered, "and not know nobody." He had never met his Uncle Joe.

"Oh, you'll make a nice lot of friends in no time," Grampa soothed him. "Let's just pretend that this is your engagement for the duration."

Mrs. Malone, letting it be known that they were leaving, sought to shield Jay from well-meaning adults. She urged that no one mention the move to him, explaining that he was unhappy about leaving all his friends.

Obliging relatives offered temporary storage for their few pieces of furniture, after which, a trunk and two traveling bags held all they had to take. Family and friends saw them off on the train, waving and shouting,

"Good-bye. Good-bye." And, "Don't forget to write often." The Bay Ferry, Jay's first ride on anything bigger than a rowboat, thrilled him so that he was all over the vessel. Finally there was another train ride, quite short, and they reached their destination after dark.

Uncle Joe met them in the dim light of the station platform. And after a hug and kiss for his sister, he took Jay's hand in his leathery palms and said warmly, "I'm right glad you've come." He was a small wiry man with a dark walrus mustache and deeply lined face. To accommodate all their luggage, he had come in the hearse. This was in fact an undertaker's vehicle with the glass top removed by somebody so they could sell it as a spring wagon. It rode most comfortably Uncle Joe said, on account of the good soft springs.

Tuckered out from his day-long excitement, Jay dozed off as the horse jogged out the dark road and his mother related the events of their trip down. Pulling up at the lane gate, they were greeted by a big excited dog, honey-color in the lantern light. "His name is Josh," Uncle Joe said. "He's a Golden Retriever, and he'll be your special friend."

For Jay it was love at first sight.

Uncle Joe let them into the big farmhouse kitchen, put down their bags and lit a lamp. Their trunk could wait for help in the morning. "Now, if you'll just set a minute while I unhitch," he said, "we'll have a little bite to eat."

Jay and his mother sank into a couple of old cozy rockers either side of a big round table cluttered with magazines and letters on top of which lay an open pair of spectacles. Facing them stood a huge, ornate "Acme Sterling" range brightly shining, and to one side, above the woodbox, hung a narrow shelf supporting two kerosene lamps and a mantel clock ornate of case and loud of tick. Cupboards about the room were crowded with china and glassware.

Uncle Joe was back in a trice and Josh came in with him. After that, Jay had eyes for nothing but his newfound friend. His thin arms encircling the eager dog's neck, he was rewarded with a lick on the cheek, which made him chuckle.

Over a quick little fire of paper and kindling wood, Uncle Joe heated up a pot of delicious soup. And he set out thick slices of homemade bread which they lathered with sweet butter. Jay paid hardly any attention to the grown-up talk, being engrossed in sneaking down to Josh tidbits much appreciated.

While Uncle Joe had a pipe, he wanted to reassure his sister that he had not asked her down just to put her to work. His eyes twinkling, he said, "You needn't to worry your head about a thing, Clara. I've got a widow-woman living clost by has been nicely handling the housekeeping."

But Mrs. Malone was not accustomed to playing the lady. She laughed, "We'll just see."

The clock struck ten and Uncle Joe laid aside his pipe. "I guess you're tired out from your trip. We'd better get some rest. There'll be time for talk in the morning."

Reminding Josh that his bed was on the porch, Uncle Joe handed the table lamp to his sister while he carried the bag they needed and led the climb up steep, narrow stairs, their shadows following along the wall.

Jay was given a small, cramped room at the head of the stairs. Its furnishings were sparse: a chipped enamel bedstead covered with a pieced quilt, one small oak bureau with matching washstand supporting suitable crockery in deep blue, one cushionless straight chair, and a pink china lamp standing on a nailkeg. This Uncle Joe lighted. With a wink he departed. Jay sat on the edge of the bed, while his mother unpacked his nightclothes, and studied his little cell. Hardly the comfy bedroom he'd left back home. But then, he would fix it up with his picture of the little drummer boy hanging there between the window and the closet door.

Tired out, he fell asleep at once. When he opened his eyes the next morning, it was at the nudge of a cold nose. Uncle Joe had sent Josh up to waken him. Hurriedly he dressed and together they ran down the stairs.

Mrs. Tarbutton, a stout cheerful woman in clean gingham, her faded hair caught in a egg-sized knot with straggling wisps, her face flushed like she'd been working over the hot stove, was saying as he entered the kitchen, "Yes, indeedy. I had eight childern myself. Six a-livin'." She beamed. "And now we're expectin' our very first gran'child."

It was a shock to Jay and his mother, learning the great distance he must travel to school—two and a half miles! What a difference after living within five blocks of the schoolhouse. But Uncle Joe hoped to pick up a secondhand bicycle somewhere at one of the farm auctions.

In those first few days, Mrs. Malone found little to do but walk about or sit with her fancy work. Mrs. Tarbutton declined her offers to help, urging her to take it easy. But the habits of a lifetime were not easily broken. Always a hard worker, Clara Malone found idleness irksome. She was not sorry when the grandbaby arrived early and Mrs. Tarbutton was needed at home.

For Jay those late summer days passed more quickly than he would ever have imagined. Helping with the chores, many of them new experiences, was fun. In his one-piece fancy stripe bathing suit that showed what a skinny little fellow he was, he worked at learning to swim. Holding his nose, he would jump off the end of the pier and dog-paddle about. Jay never did learn properly to dive. He waded the cove crabbing. And Uncle Joe took him out fishing; they started before sunup, not waiting for regular breakfast but sharing a cantaloupe out of the patch. Learning to ride the docile farm horses—Dewey and Danny—gave him a kindred feeling with Grampa Malone, though his mount hardly matched his vision of the Captain's fiery charger springing into battle. But Jay could make believe. And always Josh was there, eager for any prank his adored one might dream up.

When school started, he found good friends among some swell guys in his class. And his feud with the youngest Willey, which began when little snaggle-tooth tripped him on purpose with her jumping rope, lasted till the end of seventh grade. After their set-to, he never saw the little brat again. To his immense relief, he heard that her folks had moved away.

★ ★ ★

~

Chapter IV

That winter 1917-18 was severe as to weather. Making ready, the Tarbutton boys had hauled in for them ten two-horse wagon loads of wood. And feeding the fires in the big Acme Sterling became their endless drudgery. "One way to get warm proper," Uncle Joe allowed, "is a workout with the bucksaw." Sometimes he might keep at it way into the night by lantern light, while frigid blasts shook the woodhouse, or snow was blowing. Jay always helped, stacking neatly and keeping his uncle company with small boy talk. They discussed lots of important things,

Invariably impressed with what a fine boy Jay was, Uncle Joe worried about their prospects for Christmas that year. Those were pinching times. But kids needed Santa Claus. And he knew that Jay would be awful lonesome without his home- town friends. What could they do? He tackled his sister across the table with her knitting. Speaking softly so's not to be overheard by Jay abed, he said, "Now, Clara, you and me've got to get our heads together. What's there special that we can buy for Jay's Christmas?"

From long make-do experience, she had an answer, "You know, Joe, it's not what a child gets so much as how it looks. Wrap it fancy, hang it on a tree, and even everyday things are exciting. A new pair of stockings—he complains so about the ones I put new feet in, and gloves he needs. Them I've just about finished." She hadn't realized that a finger was off her son's old pair until the bitterly cold day they offered Mrs. Tarbutton a ride home. And Jay, his body jackknifed tightly into the buggy box, had his one finger next to frostbitten. It hurt so he was in tears.

"Well, mebbe." Uncle Joe frowned, puffing on his pipe. "But I'm of a mind to see that he gets something he don't expect. Now you help me think."

Only after a stroke of remarkable luck was he so easy in his mind that he could joke about it. He and Jay driving home in the buggy came past the abandoned log cabin, and there on the stone chimney sat a big buzzard. Uncle Joe couldn't resist a little fun, "From the looks of things, 'pears like they ain't gonna be no Christmas this year. Santa Claus must've come early and got stuck in the chimney."

Jay gave him a sideways grin. But then he began to worry. Though not a true believer, he still pretended, just to make sure he didn't hurt anybody's feelings.

Uncle Joe never stopped gloating over the power of joy he got from his good luck. On Saturday, though the weather was raw with sullen overcast threatening cold rain, he needed a quick trip to town. Jay, with Josh, had gone over to help Will Price with his boat building. And Mrs. Malone was stirring up her eggless, milkless and butterless cake.

When Joe was gone so much longer than was expected, she began to wonder what could be keeping him. And she felt some anxiety till mid-afternoon when he drove into the lane. The next thing she knew, he burst into the warm kitchen.

"Brrr," he shivered, "It's cold out there."

"Well, now you can get warm. That stove's pret' near crazy," she said, siddling past the waves of heat. "I've been bakin', is why."

He was carrying a spanking new grain bag oddly bulging. Hanging up his cap and coat, he took his easy chair by the table and drew the grain bag up between his knees. His expression was smug. She, by now ready to rest, dropped into her rocker opposite.

"I'm late," he said, "because I ran into my old friend Cap'n Roth at the hardware store. First time I'd laid eyes on him in two, three years. . . for all he don't live so fur away. He's a retired sea captain. Had quite a life travelin' all over the world. Intrustin' old feller. Now he's got him a snug little place on the water about five miles north of town. He invited us all over for some Sunday afternoon music on his phonograph."

He had brought from an inside pocket his pipe and tobacco pouch. You heard phew, phew as he cleared the stem; knock, knock of the bowl on the heel of his shoe. Two pinches of dark brown weed were tamped down, then he folded the pouch and returned it to his pocket. The flame of a splinter lit at the range was sucked into the tobacco, with one puff of smoke from the right side of his mouth, two from the left, and a cloud from his nose. Only then was he ready to satisfy his sister's curiosity.

She, meanwhile, patiently waiting, kept her eyes on the grain bag, wondering what on earth he had been up to.

"Cap'n said he was on his way to an auction, and why didn't I come along. So I went. More out of cur'osity than anything. A crowd of folks was gathered at the old Dryden place where the sale was goin' on. The Drydens are a well-to-do fam'ly hereabouts, and social folk in town. The old folks that jest passed on had lived in the same house—that'n facin' on the harbor—since they was married pret' near sixty year ago. But now they've died off and the young ones ain't wastin' no time gettin' rid of things."

Reaching into the grain bag, Joe lifted out a little military cap, dark blue cloth with gilt cord and buttons, and the kepi's top tilt.

Mrs. Malone's sweet face beamed as she turned the little treasure about in her hands. "Oh, Joe, he'll be thrilled! It's like Grampa Malone's and the little drummer boy's up in his room."

Uncle Joe chuckled. "Looks to me like it's practically brand new. Somebody took pretty good care of it, I'd say. I was lucky too. I started the biddin' at twenty-five cents, and nobody else wanted it." He dug deeper in the grain bag. "And what do you know, I got him somethin' to read besides. Wait till you see." He set on the table a package of four books tied up with twine. "I couldn't be sure what I was gettin', but they come dirt cheap."

Of the four, three dealt with American history, while the last was a picture album. Mrs. Malone began reading the titles: "Glimpses of America, Story of the Wild West by Buffalo Bill . . ."

Joe pushed the books aside. "Let's us wait on them a bit. Fer I've got some- thin' fer you, too. I've noticed, Clara, that you always think of everybody else before you think of yourself." Carefully he extracted the mysterious something that oddly bulged the grain bag. It was a lady's cape. "It's plush, the auctioneer said, and the trim is brown bear fur." He got up and brought it around the table to drape over her shoulders. "I swan, you look beautiful as a sassiety lady."

"Really, Joe?" She stroked the lustrous folds, thinking it was too nice to wear. She had a habit, whenever she received a nice gift, of declaring it "too pretty to use." And so the delicate cambric nightgowns trimmed with wide lace and pink ribbons, the handkerchiefs edged with tatting or embroidery, all the artistic little pincushions and needlecases fashioned for her by the Malone womenfolk remained tucked away, "too pretty to use." Now as she reveled in the luxurious wrap, she knew that she would probably never wear it. After all, where did she go that it would be suitable? But of course she wouldn't for the world hurt Joe's feelings.

"It commence to rain light about the time I left the Dryden house," he said, "and it worried me some that the things might get ruined. A grain bag was the quickest pertection I could think of."

"It's a beauty, Joe, and you're so sweet to think of me." She gave him an arch smile. "But you know, one thing calls for another. Like a new hat, maybe, to pretty up with that pheasant tail Aunt Martha sent me." But such talk was for her only from the teeth out.

Joe was tickled. "I thought mebbe we'd lay it away till Christmas."

Quickly, in order to have time for a peek at Jay's presents before he came home, she ran upstairs to hide the rich garment away in her bedroom.

The books, too, seemed to have had gentle usage. Inside the cover of Glimpses of America they found a folded page from a Sears, Roebuck & Co. catalogue describing the contents of each one. About this volume she read: "Portraying the complete history of the United States and Scenic America by pen and camera, representing the works of leading artists, both of the United States,

Canada and Europe. This work also contains 400 reproductions of photographs. Size 11 x 14. Bound in English silk cloth, stamped in gold. . . 98c."

And Story of the Wild West by Buffalo Bill: "A full and complete history of the renowned pioneer quartet, Boone, Crockett, Carson and Buffalo Bill. Replete with graphic descriptions of wild life and thrilling adventures by famous heroes of the frontier. A record of exciting events on the western borders pushed westward to the sea, massacres, desperate battles, extraordinary bravery, marvelous fortitude, astounding heroism, grand hunts, rollicking anecdotes, tales of sorrow, droll stories, curious escapades and a melange of incidents that make up the melodrama of civilization in its march over mountains and prairies to the Pacific. 766 pages."

Uncle Joe, listening with chin in hand, his forefinger alongside his nose, exclaimed, "Old Buffalo Bill didn't hardly leave out nothin', did he ?"

Jay's whistle in the lane startled them. He with a sweep of his arm gathered up the books; she took in hand the little cap and the grain bag. Frantically they stowed their treasures away at the back of the pantry, and were sitting sociably in their chairs when boy and dog burst in with a gust of cold air.

After supper Jay stretched out on the old leather couch, with a cushion at his head and Josh alongside, intending to read over his history lesson. History was his favorite subject, and he got good grades in it. But soon his eyes grew heavy; so his mother sent him up to bed.

As soon as they thought it was safe, his mother brought the two remaining books and read aloud what the Sears Catalogue sheet said about them.

United States Secret Service of the Late Civil War—Gen. Lafayette C. Baker "Exciting experience in the North and South, peerless adventures, hair-breadth escapes and valuable services of the detectives of the late Civil War. Fully illustrated. 480 pages."

Eagerly they searched out the last one—

Story of American Heroism. "A war gallery of noted men and events, comprising exploits of scouts and spies, forlorn hopes, hand to hand struggles, imprisonments and hair-breadth escapes, perilous journeys, terrible hardships, patient endurance, bold dashes, brilliant successes, clever captures, daring raids, wonderful achievements, magnanimous action, romantic, humorous and tragic, etc. Beautifully illustrated with over 300 original drawings."

Overwhelmed by their riches, they just stared at each other. Then on the back of an old envelope Uncle Joe added up the figures. "Better'n two thousand pages of stories and about seven hundred pictures. Now ain't that somethin'? Enough fer two winter's readin'. All fer jest a dollar."

But the heap of books there on the table seemed like maybe too much. Mrs. Malone had an idea. "What you say we just give him half for Christmas?

With his stockings and gloves, and the little cap. . . just two ought to be enough. Then the others would be good for his birthday."

"Good idee," Uncle Joe agreed. "Mebbe them last two? They sound right intrustin' to me."

She liked them too. Besides, as she leafed through one, there dropped into her lap a homemade scrapbook pasted full of the comic strip Buster Brown and his Dog Tige. She held it up.

"Are we lucky?"

Christmas morning Jay saw at a glance that Santa had not perished down the log cabin chimney. Two stockings, nicely filled, with holly sprigs in the top, hung from the clock shelf. Josh got a large meaty bone and one piece of chocolate fudge; he loved candy but it was not good for him. Jay found a big polished apple, an orange wrapped in tissue, raisin clusters and a handful of various kinds of nuts. Also, four sweets. But he was not allowed so much as one little nibble before breakfast.

Their small tree decorated with tinsel, red balls and paper angels beckoned them to the important things in packages large and small. Watching Jay unwrap his books and exclaim over them, Uncle Joe sat with his fingers laced over his stomach, absently twiddling his thumbs, "a power of joy" on his face. Santa had left him tobacco, heavy sox and handkerchiefs. Mrs. Malone found a pretty hand mirror of imitation ebony, Rose talcum powder and a subscription to the Pictorial Review. Through the mail had come a camisole with crocheted yoke for her but "too pretty to wear" and for Jay a Penny Saver bank.

As he unwrapped the military cap, sunshine spread over Jay's thin little face. Adjusting it on, he clicked his heels, gave a salute and marched across the room to the looking glass. Josh watched him quizzically,

The plush cape, folded into a clean gingham apron and carefully wrapped to appear for Jay's benefit a surprise, brought exclamations of delight. His mother draped it over her shoulders and slowly turned for them to admire. Jay capered about with excitement, shouting, "Gee, Mom, you look like a queen!" And Uncle Joe, puffing his pipe, contentedly watched their clowning.

So it had been a good Christmas after all: but tinged with sadness and longing for their absent ones. Uncle Joe could not forget last year; his sister anticipated Christmas to come when Jay's Dad would surely be home. Passing him as she tidied up, she laid her hand on his arm in wordless sympathy.

All the gift wrappings must be carefully saved. White tissues and satin ribbons would be carefully pressed with a warm iron and laid away to use again next year. Tissues from the oranges were smoothed out for toilet paper and hung on a nail out in the privy.

★ ★ ★

Chapter V

Like all patriotic Americans they were conscientious in their war sacrifices. They changed their eating habits, observing the meatless days and the wheatless days. They conserved sugar. Jay's mother seemed to be evermore knitting socks for the soldiers. Though money was awful scarce, they managed to buy a small bond during the Liberty Loan drives. They pinched every way they could. Still, they managed to be tolerably comfortable.

Letters from Jay's father told that he was not. As he said, living at the front hardly offered the comfort of his bed back home.

"I could have stayed in the dugout," he wrote, "but it was filthy. Men had lived in there too long. Overhead great thick planks support the earth. There are wide cracks between them, and you can poke a finger up into the rotten wood. Great big toadstools grow there, pretty colors—bright reds and golden yellows. Water drips in your face, and if you try to sleep, rats run over you and bite your ears and nose. I figured a shell hit would bury us and we'd smother to death before we'd be dug out; so I sleep outside."

Mostly he posted assurances that he was all right and missed them very, very much. If nothing else, he complained about the mud. Oh, Lord, the mud! When you tried to move equipment, it bogged down, immovable for men and animals together, sunk in the mire up to their knees. There was no use to beat the poor beasts; they couldn't go nowhere.

He lamented the devastation and the sad plight of the refugees, thankful that his loved ones were safe from all the horror. Always he tried to keep them cheerful.

"Up at the front," he wrote, "I found a can. Finding that can meant that I could take a bath. It was a large can. So I went down to the canal and filled it full of water. Then I kindled me a fire, laid some stones around, and put on my can of water. When it was warm I washed up. Then I got it boiling and put in my clothes, I knew that boiling water alone wouldn't kill lice; you have to add salt. I got some salt. When my clothes were clean I put them on. I had a hard time because they had shrunk. That cheap wool they use. But I managed to get into them. They had a million wrinkles. Ay gorsh, I thought I was the only soldier so near the front without any lice.

"But before long I reached down to my ribs and brought him out. There he was. And suddenly I realized how come. We wear our dog tags on a tape. I forgot to boil the tape. When I unrolled it, there they were, a zillion of them, just like horses in a stable, all lined up in a row."

Things like that he wrote, little stories you remembered with a chuckle.

After his hay-time mishap, Jay went through a long spell of moodiness that Uncle Joe considered unnatural for any normal boy his age. It was very troubling. The old gent cudgelled his brain: how to keep the lad occupied and entertained through the summer. When his rheumatism had flared up, he was finally persuaded to let the Tarbutton boys farm his place on shares. But he and Jay took care of the stock, did the milking and kept up with the garden chores. When they worked together, weeding or maybe picking potato bugs, he often tried through innocent remarks to learn what was eating his nephew. He never could find out.

For quite a while they had been needing a new rowboat. But none reasonable enough had turned up at auction. Then, deep in a sleepless night, the idea visited Uncle Joe: he and Jay would build a boat. That was the ticket!

Over his breakfast pancakes he said, "How'd you like to help me build us a boat?"

Jay grinned. "Sure!"

"You got some experience helpin' Will Price with his." (Privately he reckoned Jay's contribution had amounted to little more than fetch and carry, with a deal of chatter, which old man Price seemed to find entertaining). "And I could use some first-rate ideas." He was secretly congratulating himself on his cleverness.

First off, they must decide on the place where they wanted to work. The old wagon shed was not bad for space and they'd be under cover. To make ready took nearly a whole day for clearing accumulations of stuff stored in there. In the afternoon, Jay, going about barefoot, stepped on an old rusty nail. His mother, terrified of lockjaw, applied her turpentine remedy: warm to the wound, cold to the face and neck, then gently rubbed along the spine. To keep Jay's mind occupied, Uncle Joe talked boat. "Mornin', noon and night," his sister said. They worked on plans for size and style (Jay had a knack for drawing pictures), carefully figured quantity and cost of materials they could afford, calculated any new tools they might be needing. It was agreed that they'd not hurry the work but go slowly. This job must be equal to anything turned out by the regular boatbuilders in town.

Through the summer days she gradually took shape, their neat little craft, pristine white with trim a medium brown wood color. She drew compliments from everyone who saw her. And Jay went around bursting with pride. The shine in his eyes brought joy to his elders.

One day Uncle Joe opened a subject that nestled in the back of his mind. "Have you give thought yet to what we'll be callin' her?" He knew already. But it must be Jay's idea.

"No, Sir."

"Well, now, it's high time we figgered on it. Don't you think so? You got any best girls with pretty names?" He fixed his nephew with a stern look over his glasses.

Jay grinned bashfully and shook his head,

Uncle Joe thought differently. "Sure you've got a best girl." He waited, busy filling his pipe.

Jay considered. Suddenly light dawned. "Mom!"

"Of course. We'll call her the Clarabelle. There ain't no prettier name this side the pearly gates."

So they put their heads together drawing stencils for the neatest of lettering. No town boatbuilder was going to find fault with their work.

The Tarbutton boys helping, they brought their treasure down to the pier. Mrs. Malone, standing with her hands folded under her apron, exclaimed over her namesake. And Josh, who had supervised the whole project from his place just inside the wagon- shed doors, capered about, barking excitedly.

Thankful for the miracle of Jay's restored good spirit, his mother looked fondly upon his boat. On her way to the henhouse or the hogpen, she always glanced "seaward" to admire the little beauty out there resting on its reflection. And when her menfolks set forth on their first fishing trip, she watched the trim little craft skimming smoothly over the water, oars dipping and rising, bearing the "fellows," in new overalls and old straw hats, out to the deeps of the creek. They made a picture, and she thought, "If only I had a camera."

Towards the end of August, the old Spencer place on the island was rented to a family from New York named Williams. Nothing much was known about them. A lawyer, Mr. Williams had to give up his offices because of failing eyesight and poor health. Mrs. Williams in times past was a singer on the stage. And they had a young daughter.

Spencer's island once upon a time formed the tip of the peninsula. But erosion had cut that small parcel of land adrift. Now its only connection with the point was a narrow causeway of oyster shells, not too deep even during flood for a horse and buggy crossing, but traversed on foot only at low tide. The tall old frame house, weathered and gaunt, had stood empty for some time, and the whole place, long untended, was wildly overgrown.

Why these big city folks chose to settle down here puzzled everyone. But nothing of their affairs would be learned from any of the family. They were all close-mouthed. It was made quite plain that they intended to live in seclusion. Old man Blades had been hired to fetch their mail and do their marketing. If they needed a trip to town, they would go in his boat.

Though the new folks appeared uppity, Mrs. Malone remarked that their lamp light across the water "seemed right neighborly." And after a proper interval, she put on her good dress and paid a polite call. About her impressions she was mum, never expressing in Jay's hearing her opinion of Mrs. Williams. Their young daughter, she said, was "a sweet little creature".

The newcomers were hardly settled before school started and Marta Williams appeared in Jay's class. She was just beginning eighth grade, as was he.

Shortly afterward, when he caught sight of her walking the road one morning, he waved and called, "Wait and I'll go with you."

As usual, Josh gamboled along beside him as far as the gate, where Marta stood leaning against a post, her strapped books over one shoulder, an orange lunch box in her hand. Dark honey blonde, she had big brown eyes and a nice smile showing small even white teeth. Her crisp sky-blue hair bow matched the tie of her gray middy blouse. Josh got his parting pat on the head and forlornly watched them leave, his tail wagging slower, slower and sagging until it was still.

Already a bit late, they knew they had to step on it. Marta told Jay that she would be rowing across the cove and walking in each day. They agreed to make the trip together. In spite of hurrying, they had not quite reached the outskirts of town when they heard the school bell sounding across the flat farmland. With a gasp of dismay, Jay caught Marta by the hand and they began to run. Though she was a palely plump young lady, she managed to keep up.

In the afternoon, trudging home they had time for improving their acquaintance. And Jay could share with Marta his dread of the cutoff through the woods. About half way to town, it might save you a quarter mile walk, dare you use it. But it was a scary place. More so on dark days. Beginning at a blasted tree with an osprey's ruined stick nest in the top, the narrow track snaking over matted pine needles, low in spots with standing dark water, disappeared into the dense pine woods. Jay had tried this shortcut once. He started in blithely enough, but only a little way along, fear gripped him. He began to feel terribly alone, surrounded by a sinister silence and gloom. In panic he turned and ran back out. After that, walking the road, he hurried past. And in the buggy during the drive home after a picture show, it seemed that Dewey, even at a trot, was too poky slow passing through the pitch black stretch of close woods.

Listening in on the conversations of his elders, he had learned that a crazy man escaped from an asylum was hiding out somewhere in the countryside. A farm woman driving alone claimed to have seen him asleep beside a log, but at the time she told nobody. Jay's fears multiplied. He never heard that the person was captured. But to be on the safe side, as he explained to Marta, it was safest to keep on the far side of the road, hoping to see nothing more terrifying than the brooding woods.

★ ★ ★

Chapter VI

News of the Armistice sped over the wires before daylight that Monday morning, November 11, 1918. The church bells rang, and the town went wild. People forgot everything. They surged through the streets, blowing horns and whistles. They fired off guns. Marta being kept home with a bad cold, Jay rode into school that day so he could pick up a few supplies. Reaching town he encountered such jubilation as made even placid Dewey skittish. Nobody had time for school; there would be a holiday. But Jay hung around awhile with the crowd gathered to hang the Kaiser in effigy. That over, he tore himself away. They'd want the great news at home.

Dewey trotted briskly out of town, but slowed to a walk once they passed the depot. Jay, lost in daydreams of his Dad's homecoming that would soon whisk him back to the old home place, left Dewey to follow his own lead. Inattentive to all but his thoughts, he rocked along, the reins draped loosely over his mount's neck. Once again he would be leading the junior fighting forces in screaming assault along the towpath. With him so long away, the fort must need a lot of repairs. The fellows had probably let the place go to pot. He saw himself again marching in the parades on Decoration Day; though it wouldn't be quite the same now with Dad Seltzer and Mr. Bricker both gone.

Ambling along thusly, they were less than half way home when a big Collie dog suddenly stepped out of the nearby woods and startled Dewey. With a snort the big brute sidestepped his forefeet right into the ditch, and Jay pitched headforemost down over his roached mane. Unhurt, the boy scrambled up, shouting, "Whoa!" But the heedless Dewey took off for home. And Jay was left to follow on foot, lugging his schoolbooks and the bag of supplies which had fallen off with him. Soon he found his saddle blanket in the middle of the road, And further along, there lay the saddle.

When Dewey showed up riderless at the farm gate, Uncle Joe's strength almost failed him. Expecting the worst, he hopped aboard bareback and pushed the wayward rascal at a gallop back to town. Great was his relief to meet the luckless Jay trudging along under the weight of his belongings. And he could hardly smother his mirth when he heard what had happened.

War's end brought back to Mrs. Malone's face, almost as of old, the little smile that even in repose lingered about her dark eyes and the corners of her mouth, as if she were pleased with what she saw or what she might be thinking. Dimmed by heart-ache during the long months past, it shone again. Her thoughts, and Jay's, dwelt upon their return home. Yet that was not mentioned. As she cautioned Jay, they must wait until Dad returned, and that might take some time yet. Meanwhile, to herself she worried about leaving Brother Joe alone.

John Jay Malone II was twice wounded and returned to the battle lines. Then, just two weeks before the war ended, they found only his dog tag.

Mrs. Malone took the news bravely. She was not a weeper in front of others. Jay sat stunned. Their sorrow deeply troubled good, kind Uncle Joe. He said gently, "You know, Clara, you and Jay always have a home here."

His mother's meaningful glance silenced Jay. She said, "You're mighty good to us, Joe. We'll try to make it up to you."

And as time passed, she noticed that Joe, bless his heart, tried to make it up to them. The poor man never spent money on himself. But he kept in mind their need for a little pleasure. The picture show right often was his idea. And he liked to pick out a little bag of fancy candies at the Greek Candy Store so that Clara might enjoy a treat she didn't have to fix herself.

For some time Uncle Joe had talked peach orchard. Just a small one. But it must be a planting of the choicest fruit. Not only was he very fond of peaches—"You know, Clara, just thinking 'big juicy peach' makes my mouth water"—but also he considered the prospects good for a profitable market later on. The field he intended to use was bordered by a growth of cedar trees, some old and hoary, others young. Naturally they would have to go. The big ones, sawed up, might make a nice chest for woolens and such. "One of them little 'uns," he said, "is just about right fer a proper Christmas tree." He and his sister had decided that even though their hearts were not in it, still there should be Christmas for Jay.

Cold rain rattled on the windows, but their evening was cozy, the three of them gathered around the big table: Uncle Joe at ease in his comfort chair, his slippered feet resting on the hassock, Mrs. Malone opposite and busy with her mending, Jay sharing with Josh the leather couch.

Jay had an idea. "How about if we could sell some of the little ones? Folks'll want Christmas trees, same as us. I could take a few orders maybe, and Marta'll help."

Uncle Joe valued gumption in young people. "A capital idee!" He took a couple of puffs on his pipe. "Tell you what. We'll be partners. You take the orders. And I'll help han'le the delivery. Trees are a mite awkard to unload. You and Marta can divide the money. And I'll get my grove cleared away. How's that?"

His sister smothered a smile, thinking, "Only brother Joe could offer such a scheme without blushing."

His impish sideways glance told her that he knew what she was thinking.

Jay was immensely pleased. But sharing the good news with Marta would have to keep till Monday schooltime. After his first few visits he had given up going over to the island. He felt unwanted there. The place gave him the willies, and Marta's parents were so odd. He never saw Mr. Williams. Mrs. Williams he knew only through a window screened with vines. And no matter what he and Marta might be doing—like planting the Grave Privet—her mother kept jawing at them, and Marta went right on with what she was about, paying not the slightest attention, quite indifferent. Even when "the old lady" fell silent, which seemed all too rarely, he had the uncomfortable feeling that she spied on them, grim and disapproving.

From the first, Marta had prattled about a flower garden. She kept remembering Grandmama's back home. One afternoon when she and Jay were crossing the old family burying ground out back of the house, Marta caught the loose sole of her shoe in a creeper and fell down. Jay gave her a hand up.

"What is this stuff?" she asked with a sweep of her arm across the wide reaches of green leaves.

"It's Grave Privet. When it blooms, this whole place is covered with blue flowers."

"Oh, blue is my favorite color." She clapped her hands. "Can I have some?"

"Sure. You can have all you want."

"Right now?"

"M'm," reluctantly. Then with a shrug, "Sure. We'll need to find a shovel. And a basket."

That day, Mrs. Williams seemed even more aggravating than usual, if that were possible. And Jay made up his mind—never again.

But Marta could always count on a warm welcome from his folks. They quickly came to love her like a daughter. Happily the little girl accepted their house as her second home. And very soon it seemed quite natural to include her in everything.

Saturdays the two of them shared the buggy with his mother on her trips to town because she enjoyed their company so. Then, while she shopped, they had time to explore and spend a few cents of their own money. After school, with so much ground to cover, they dare not tarry for long, especially during the short days of winter. But weekends they could indulge their little interests. From the hitching rack they scattered their separate ways.

Marta made a beeline for the small gift shop with red geraniums in the window, and oftentimes the owner's black cat asleep in the sunshine. She enjoyed there a warm friendship with the ancient lady who never hurried her in choosing another of those dinky little flowered doilies she was forever embroidering. Along with that three penny purchase, she selected six chocolate creams that melted in your mouth. They ate them while jogging home. Her parents never cared for sweets.

Jay liked to look through the hardware store that smelled of rubber "and things"; maybe choose a new ball or a few marbles. Then he might wander toward the boat yards or, lured by the clang of the blacksmith's hammer, go and watch a horse being shod.

But now the time was growing short; they must attend to their Christmas tree business. Going door to door of the neat houses bordering the side streets, they hardly realized what a woeful pair they looked, poor patched country kids peddling their fresh-cut Christmas trees at twenty-five cents each. Orders in hand, they were eager for the cutting, which absorbed their whole attention until finally the hearse was loaded and with Uncle Joe driving, they set out in high spirits. The responsibilities were divided: Jay would ring the doorbells and hand over the tree; Marta would take the money, which she carried in her pocketbook. They were dressed for the season, Jay wearing his new red scarf, rosy-cheeked Marta in a red coat and hood made for her Christmas present by Mrs. Malone.

After they'd had chance to count the settlement in full, Jay and Marta swaggered about, proud of their jinglings in the pocket. How wonderful to be rich! And they knew exactly what they intended to buy. Ice skates. Ordered now, they would be on hand for great fun when Marta got back from spending the holidays with her Grandmama in Washington City.

Though his elders tried on Jay's account to make Christmas as happy as possible, it was quiet. Their little tree prettily displayed the paper angels and strings of red holly berries. Underneath Jay found a stag-handle pocket knife (to replace his that got lost), and a book that Uncle Joe picked up someplace called Hot Stuff by Famous Funny Men. A collection of stories by such writers as Mark Twain, Josh Billings, Bill Nye, Petroleum V. Nasby, Artemus Ward, Bret Harte, and the like, it was packed full of humor, wit, satire, ridicule, repartee, anecdotes, bulls and blunders. Uncle Joe smiled over his sox and tobacco (he got the same each year), and Mrs. Malone unwrapped handmade gifts as usual "too pretty to use."

★ ★ ★

Chapter VII

With the New Year, school started. But where was Marta? Jay waited for her till the last moment, then went on to town alone. Each morning he expected to see her. For a whole week he was disappointed. Going it alone, the trip seemed interminable. The road stretched away, long and empty and lonesome. There was no lively camaraderie to warm the spirits. She didn't come, and didn't come. They wondered why.

Then one morning there she was! A sight for sore eyes, as Uncle Joe would say. Bundled up in her red coat and hood, she was waiting at the gate. Jay and Josh broke into a run. In his rapture the dog almost knocked her down.

She was all agog. "Have they come? The skates?"

"Yep."

"You didn't begin without me?" She pretended to pout.

"Course not. I've been waiting. Where you been all this time?"

"Grandmama needed me to help her nurse poor Purvey. He's her parrot. He's real, real old. He kept saying, 'Purvey's hungry. Purvey's hungry.' We were so worried. But we finally got him filled up. Then he laughed."

Though she was late, smart little Marta quickly made up her missed lessons. Jay, inclined to laziness, was glad to occasionally consult her about classwork. Sometimes he felt a twinge of jealousy bearing constant praise of Marta's cleverness. "She's the brightest child and catches on so quickly," his mother would remark after they had figured how to make some intricate fancywork pattern, or Marta picked out a tune on their old piano. Though lessons had been denied her, she could play by ear remarkably well.

But he never said anything, and his irritation soon passed. Marta was such a good sport. If he dared, she dared. And when he was afraid, she trembled with him. In all things she accepted his judgment without question. Such absolute faith nourished his self-esteem, made him feel big and important.

When his mother firmly ruled out the frozen edges of the creek as too treacherous, they skated on a shallow ice-covered pond in the woods. And from supporting each other, with many falls and much laughter, they developed skill in skimming through the sticks protruding. Their antics gave Josh fits.

Success with the Christmas trees encouraged thoughts of other lucrative ventures. And they began shaping ambitious plans. Soon would come the season for huckleberries which they could peddle at twelve and a half cents a quart to the nice fat German lady who lived on a farm near the edge of town. And they had big ideas about how many baskets of tomatoes they could pick.

Marta might look delicate, but she was tough. And Jay respected her courage. He could count on her to join in any scheme, no matter how daring. And if things went wrong, she was no cry-baby.

Only once did he see her cry. Not when they were picking blackberries and a wasp stung her on the upper lip. Nor when she slipped and struck her big painful stone bruise on a sharp stob. Not even when the water moccasin suddenly slithered from the mud between her ankles. It happened when she was given a sad poem to read in a program at school:

"That poor little boy with no cap on his head,

A board is his bed, his mother is dead,

That poor little boy with no cap on his head,

Has never a friend in the world."

Marta got so far and broke down, crying into her blue bow tie. Quickly the teacher consoled her, and later asked her to read another piece that was happier.

In after years, thinking back to those days, Jay wondered: could it be that Marta, who bore up so staunchly under physical adversity, had associated the verse's tragedy with himself and his mother, whom she dearly loved?

He knew that Marta would deny herself if he were in need. But for her, he would have gone hungry that day at school when he left his lunch box on a window sill in the ivy-mantled bell tower, and at noontime found his ham sandwich and chocolate cake full of ants. Marta made him take half of her skimpy cheese sandwich and a ginger cookie.

And when his mother had one of her sick headaches, Marta hovered about, soothing her brow with soft hands and cool moist cloths, afterwards gently combing her long black hair.

Severe sore throat kept Marta home that Arbor Day. And Jay was late picking up his tree. Handing over his two cents, he took the only thing left— a dead-looking switch that had lost its identification tag. Somebody thought it was a peach. Oh, well, he and Marta would do their bit planting it, out of sight in a far corner of his own garden patch.

Sight of the sad thing tickled her immensely. But they pitched in, digging deep for its tiny root ball. Marta said, "I'll just think a little prayer for it."

Daily they watered it, hoping, but not expecting anything. When at last they found a tiny green leaf, they danced a jig.

A couple of report cards that anybody could be proud of were their passports to lazy summer days. For roughing it, they dressed alike; over blue bathing suits each pulled on a pair of old brown pants (Marta's on loan). Barefoot, they wore on their heads, when they remembered, wide-brimmed straw hats.

They went beachcombing, poking through the driftwood left helter-skelter and draped with tatters of seaweed. Marta found half buried in the sand a broken barpin of faceted black glass which she treasured in her trinket box kept hidden under the hay in their barn. Jay discovered a homemade toy boat washed up from who knows what perilous voyage, still carrying its little crooked sail.

They hunted birds' eggs for his collection. Never more than one was taken from a nest. And he displayed them in a box lined with milkweed floss, all neatly labeled. One day they found a hole in the high bank along the shore —a kingfisher's nest. When he recklessly thrust in his hand and was nipped by a sharp beak, Marta danced with glee. Shamefaced, he grinned back at her.

Later, when she crammed a fistful of red raspberries into her mouth and gagged on a stink bug, he nearly split his sides laughing.

Her good-nature was contagious. They might argue, sometimes vehemently, but they never really quarreled. He was usually tolerant of her girlish whims, while she strove to keep pace with his he-man ventures.

When not roughing it, Marta indulged her high-flown ideas of fashionable living. Though Jay preferred other pastimes to games of housekeeping, he humored her imaginings if nothing more exciting offered. When she required a house, he obliged, arranging logs in the woodshed to enclose her parlor. Their inevitable tea party was satisfying as to cold biscuits with jelly, but he balked at lukewarm cambric tea.

So that she might regally ride out in her carriage, they rigged up his red wagon with a top-heavy cover of tow sacks. Jay was always the horse, of course. One afternoon he accidentally upset her in the ditch. Untangling herself from the canopy and lap-robe, Marta came up scolding. But seeing his shocked surprise, she burst out laughing, helped him right the unwieldy conveyance, and calmly resumed her drive.

Through the long summer days they shared whatever games they could think up, inventing their own entertainment. No one their age came to visit. Yet they remained ever hopeful. Whenever a moving object in a small cloud of dust appeared up the road, they, like any backwoodsy folks, climbed to the porch railing, eager to see who was coming. But few and far between were signs of life in the direction of town.

Near time for the Floating Theater to dock, his mother invited Marta to see a play. And the little girl was thrilled to her fingertips. She could talk of nothing else. Thinking about it, she would murmur, "Oh, this is the most exciting thing in my whole life!"

At once there was much ado about what she should wear. The pretty blue mull dress his mother had started, of course. One last fitting and it would be ready. But what about shoes?

Because she was so hard on footwear (after all, twenty miles a week over oyster shell roads scuffed a lot of shoe leather), Marta's parents bought for her heavy boy's shoes. And added copper toes! Those horrid shoes were the bane of her existence. Now she wailed, "A beautiful dress with old ugly clodhoppers!" And unhappiness troubling her gentle soul suddenly mushroomed into rebellion. She would have a pair of lady's shoes. She could buy them with her own money—nickels and dimes hard-earned through hot noons in the berry patches where the chiggers nearly ate you alive, and backbreaking hours filling countless baskets of tomatoes. And she intended to have exactly what she wanted. Her fever of anxiety was calmed only by a trip with Mrs. Malone to the shoe store.

When the eagerly anticipated day came, Uncle Joe, handing them up into the buggy, said, "You both look beautiful." With a satisfied smile Marta smoothed the soft folds of her blue skirt and peeked down at her strapped slippers. She put on more airs than an heiress, Jay thought grumpily, his nose out of joint at being left behind. Sliding down the barn roof, which was forbidden, he had sprained his ankle.

Marta came home bubbling with rapture and wonder. The actresses were so enchanting that she had decided on her future then and there: she would act the heroine of a beautiful story. And one of the actors was ever so good-looking, with his black, black hair and white, white teeth. Her thoughts and prattle skipped from the characters, the clothes, the music, the flowers, to a happening altogether puzzling. How could big snowflakes fall on the stage when outside it was still summertime?

She sighed. "This is the most exciting day of my life!" Dancing a little pirouette and watching the swirl of her full skirt, she danced over and gave Mrs. Malone a kiss, saying, "Thank you, thank you."

School brought an end to their barefoot freedom and Marta faced again those hated copper toes. But she got sick. And Jay learned that she would not be returning. Mr. Williams was seriously ill and needed specialized care; so they were leaving.

Screwing up his willpower, Jay walked over to say good-bye to Marta. Her mother greeted him from the window behind the vines. "Marta's not well enough to see anybody right now. But I'll tell her you came by."

He shuffled his feet, intimidated, but hoping for one last word with Marta. "We'll miss her," he managed to say.

"I'll tell her," old stony-heart replied.

"Mother sent over the paper dolls that Marta likes." He held out the Journal.

"Just leave it on the steps," she told him.

A moment longer he hesitated, then placing the magazine on the nearest corner of the bottom step, he disconsolately turned away.

From the edge of their woods he looked back at the tall gray house rising against overcast sky. There, framed in a small bull's-eye window high up in the peak of the roof, was Marta's face and her little hand waving. With a thrill of pleasure he answered her. And for a long minute they waved to each other. Reluctantly, he started away, then turned back for another lingering farewell. Abruptly he wheeled and fled down the lane between their tall gloomy pines. The tide was rising. High-stepping through the deepening water, he ran across the causeway.

★ ★ ★

Chapter VIII

With the loss of little Marta, Uncle Joe began to worry. He dreaded that Jay's despondency following his haytime accident might return. Ahead stretched Autumn days and the long, lonesome walks to and from school. It might save the situation if Jay could ride Dewey, but livery stable charges were steep. The prices on bicycles dismayed him. He asked around that everybody be on the lookout for a second-hand bike. The Methodist minister happened upon what he needed and could pay for. Though a month early for Jay's sixteenth birthday, that was his present. And he was so thrilled.

Then, before Uncle Joe had time to replenish the till, he splurged again. So that Jay and his mother might glimpse the wide, restless ocean, he stretched his purse to buy tickets for a train excursion to Ocean City. It seemed to Jay that the day would never come. Eager to help make ready, he got so underfoot that his mother finally gave him the task of neatly packing their two small picnic hampers. They would feast on sandwiches of ham and chicken, pickled eggs, cherry tarts and chocolate layer cake. The sight of such goodies tempted Jay to sample with the tip of his finger the frosting on his piece of cake.

Admonishing Josh to look after things, they gaily set forth, plenty early, in the motor boat. Pulling out into the cove, Jay couldn't bear to look back at his pal there on the end of the pier dejectedly watching them leave without him. Chugging around the point through the narrows, they turned up Back Creek. Almost within sight of their destination, the motor died. Uncle Joe frantically tinkered with it. Nothing worked. The moments ticked away. They heard the train blow. It stopped and they could picture a flock of eager people climbing aboard. Soon with clang and clamor it pulled out, gathering steam as it sped away past them up along the shoreline. Meanwhile, there they sat out on the water, with their full picnic baskets, dolefully watching it go without them.

They were stalled just about in front of Price's. Old Will came out to offer help and towed them in to his pier. Then, everybody in the dismals, they plodded home across the fields. Mrs. Malone tried to keep up, but her menfolks strode along so fast, angrily kicking any clods in their path, that she finally quit trying. Stopping to catch her breath, she laughed. Such dour faces! "Oh, come, you two, this isn't world's end." They grinned sheepishly. She said, "We'll just have a nice picnic at home."

Their absence had lasted less than a couple of hours; yet Josh greeted them like they'd been gone forever. Jay's disappointment was the dog's joy, for he shared the sandwiches.

A delayed present for Jay's Christmas that year was a small box camera that his mother got with Octagon Soap. It came five weeks late because of the time she needed to collect enough coupons. Kindhearted Mrs. Tarbutton contributed some. "Here, take mine," she said. "I've saved 'em but I don't know fer what." And Uncle Joe went to the expense of buying extra soap to make up the count. It was his idea to begin with, after he came across a box of coupons on a high pantry shelf.

At first Jay snapped everything in sight, willy-nilly, getting mostly pictures that were awful: Uncle Joe dunging out the stable, his mother at the hog pen, her face half hidden by the shirred hood of her bonnet. Josh figured largely, but too far away or blurred in motion. Then the boy began to realize that he couldn't afford to be wasteful of film. Neither could he expect his magic box to produce a fine photograph of any scene he had given only a cursory glance. He learned to be choosy about his backgrounds, to be critical of the picture he would preserve.

Diligently he worked at refining his ideas of composition and mood, using for one subject a scene that had long intrigued him. In a gut through wide marsh at the far end of Uncle Joe's fields, a Chesapeake Bay skipjack, the Fanny L. Benton, was "laid up for dead." She still carried her mast and boom and wheel, her bowsprit pointing seaward toward the scenes of her heyday. Once trim and neat, her paint had become scurfy, her iron coated with rust. Jay and Josh first approached her by rowboat, maneuvering for just the right angle to express her sadness against stormy sky. Another day, as a snowstorm commenced, his camera stopped time, fixing forever that melancholy moment of her inexorable dissolution.

His camera helped him bear bitter disappointment at being left behind when his mother went home for Grampa Malone's funeral. Jay begged her to bring back pictures of everybody, and she took along one of him on Dewey. Trying to control his tears, he sent a message to the fellows: "Tell everybody I said, 'Hi!'"

Grampa was buried in his Grand Army uniform, with one of his two large flags draped over the casket. The church soloist sang When The Roll Is Called Up Yonder. His other flag and his service pistol he left to Jay when he should come of age. People remarked that Decoration Day would never be the same, now that only two old soldiers were left and they growing ever feebler.

Though never a real robust lad, from the first Jay was a big help on the farm. Obedient and polite, accustomed to doing his chores, he had made himself useful in many ways. Depending upon the season, he (with Marta) searched out wild asparagus along the line fences, picked berries and fruit, even plums from the ancient damson trees along the lane. But they were a wormy lot. He hoed the big garden, and helped his mother tend her flowers, marveling at her preference for a large waxy white rose with no more scent than a tallow candle.

So that the boy's sense of responsibility and pride be nourished by property exclusively his own, Uncle Joe gave him a small fertile garden plot, and half a dozen fine hens with a big bossy rooster. With each hatching of chicks he acquired a nice enlargement of his flock. They left high-stepping Jenny Hen clucking over ten little peeps the cloudless Sunday afternoon they drove over for a musical treat at Captain Roth's.

The Captain was a cheery rotund little man with blue eyes, a snowy fringe around his bald spot and a trim mustache to match. He shared his small white frame house with a dozen or so complacent cats—mostly orange, but some black and a couple of tigers. Mrs. Malone remarked that the place was "neat as a pin." The Captain heartily greeted them, saying, "Welcome, my friends!" shaking hands all around, receiving Jay as cordially as if he were an adult. He ushered them into his parlor. Small and cozy, it contained, besides the polished Victrola, reed chairs with brown corduroy cushions for the comfort of all his guests, as well as a footstool for young people like Jay. The room's chief ornament was a gold hanging lamp decorated with painted flower designs in natural colors and encircled by a wealth of cut glass pendants. And on the stiffly starched lace curtains were pinned paper butterflies.

The old gentleman talked proudly of his large record collection. There was entertainment for all ages. Blissfully he listened, hands clasped over his pot belly, a smile on his face, occasionally closing his eyes and nodding in time with the music. Conversation was not encouraged during the program. But they chatted while changing records and during an intermission for refreshments of ice cream and cake. Mrs. Malone complimented him on his flower beds, and they shared the lore of plants.

Learning that the talking machine cost less than he had imagined, Uncle Joe decided that they should begin to save for one. And perhaps now was the time to make notes on the records they liked. The gospel hymns stirred him, especially a male quartet offering When The Roll Is Called Up Yonder, and a soprano/contralto duet of Whispering Hope.

Mrs. Malone was charmed by a tenor singing Silver Threads Among the Gold. But she would be long haunted by the instrumental pieces: A Perfect Day beautifully rendered by violin, 'cello and piano, and The Sweetest Story Ever Told blending violin, flute and harp.

Intriguing to all of them was something different, clever whistling of Spring Voices.

Jay responded with merriment to the comic songs such as Waltz Me Around Again Willie, Waiting At The Church and a tenor solo of troubles with The Whole Damn Family.

Entertained as never before, they forgot the time. A clock off in the house somewhere faintly striking reminded Uncle Joe to consult his watch, and he was shocked to find it already four in the afternoon. His sister, observing him, leaned forward in her chair and said, with her usual grace, "It's been delightful, Captain, and I'm afraid we've overstayed. We really must be going."

"Thank you all for coming." The Captain gave them a little bow. "For me the afternoon has just melted away. We must do this again."

"And you must come visit us," Mrs. Malone said. "Try one of our Pennsylvania dinners."

Because the music so enraptured them, they had been deaf to the rumble of distant thunder. Now they stepped out on the porch to face ominous black clouds shot with lightning and rapidly rolling in from the west.

The Captain insisted they wait out the storm. "'My friends, I won't let you go. Come quickly, Laddie, and we'll shelter your good horse in the barn." He plucked his cap from the hall-tree, and they ran out to move Dewey from under the tall oak tree already rocking in strong wind.

Uncle Joe looked doubtful, but his sister reassured him. She had thought to close all the windows. Besides, it hardly made sense to start now; they'd never make it home ahead of the storm.

When everybody was again seated in the parlor, Jay politely asked if he might hear Billy Murray sing The Whole Damm Family once more. He wanted to memorize it.

The Captain said, "Oh, but you must take notes." And besides providing pad and pencil, he obligingly stood by the machine to stop the record while Jay, jotting down the lines, was able to catch up:

"Last summer at a watering place, a man named Damm I met/ Who entertained me with such grace, said I, 'Now don't forget./ Next winter come and visit me.' Said he, 'That's what I'll do.'/ And yesterday that man arrived and brought some others too./

"There was Mr. Damm and Mrs. Damm, the Damm kids two or three./ With You be Damm and I be Damm, and the whole Damm family./

"My apartment is a small affair. Just room for two or three./ Since that Damm family landed here, there is no room for me./ The rooms are full of different Damms of every size and shape./ So with the Damm dog I must sleep out on the fire escape./

"There is Mr. Damm and Mrs. Damm, the Damm kids two or three./ With You be Damm and I be Damm, and the whole Damm family."

Suddenly in the doorway appeared an enormous orange cat. He looked up and opened his mouth but no sound came out. The Captain looked down and opened his mouth but said nothing. "Poor Midas has lost his voice," he explained. "And he's deaf too. But we communicate." He crooked his forefinger and the cat came over to be lifted into the old gentleman's scant lap. Just then a shoot of sunshine through the butterflies on the lace curtains glorified the animal's fur and announced the storm's passing. It had been quick, leaving behind raindrop diamonds sparkling on the shrubbery, and a short, faint rainbow.

But jogging toward home, they found increasing evidence of violence. Debris of tree limbs and foliage was strewn everywhere. Wind and rain had wreaked havoc. The lane gate had become unhinged. Their ancient willow, uprooted, lay stretched across the yard. Low places were flooded. And there in the ditch water floated Jenny Hen's baby chicks, drowned, all but one.

★ ★ ★

Chapter IX

Uncle Joe never quite got over his disappointment that they failed to make the excursion to Ocean City. It troubled him on Jay's account. Hard times or not, the boy should have some happy memories. And after they got the Ford, he determined to try again.

He accepted the car in place of money so long owed him that he had chalked it off as a bad debt. Turning into the lane, he chuckled at the surprise of Jay and his mother.

"Step in," he invited them, "and we'll go for a little drive."

His sister demurred. "But, Joe, we look a fright."

"Never mind. We won't go far, and we'll keep to the back roads."

Without further thought, they climbed in just as they were: she in her old everyday work dress, her hair straggly, and Jay wearing a tattered shirt with his most disreputable scuff pants. Excited, feeling like millionaires, they chugged out the sparsely populated long point road, away from town, where they'd not likely meet anybody they knew. How exhilarating it was!

Then, deep in the country, the car stopped, giving everybody near heart-failure. They had run out of gas. Jay's mother was mortified that he had to trudge into town for a can of gasoline to roll them home.

"Well, that'll be a lesson to me," Uncle Joe said, disgusted with himself. "You can bet that I won't let it happen again."

For Jay the car was a great toy. He liked to go in the wagon shed and just sit in it—the seats were softer than those in the buggy—imagining himself out on the road with admiring friends.

The first opportunity, Uncle Joe announced that they would drive to Ocean City. Mrs. Malone just looked askance at him. Jay shouted, "Oh, boy!"

They left the house about daylight, covering familiar roads before sunup, then divided their time between admiring the pleasant landscape and making sure that Uncle Joe took the right turns. To Mrs. Malone the long trip was tiring. But Jay's excitement never waned until they pulled onto the edge of the sand beach and looked upon the breakers rolling in. Uncle Joe said, "Now that's a sight for sore eyes."

Parking at a spot where nobody else happened to be around, they fastened up the car curtains for privacy in quickly slipping into their bathing suits. The hours passed in joyous frolic, splashing in the surf, beachcombing for fancy shells, and Jay building an elaborate sand fort. They relished their picnic lunch spread out on a red checked table cloth. The day was perfect, except that Jay's camera somehow got left at home. So they dallied a little longer than they intended.

Ready to leave, they found the car stuck in the sand. With Uncle Joe behind the steering wheel, and Jay and his mother both pushing, still it was only after a helpful stranger lent his brawn that they finally got rolling.

A few miles out of town they had a flat tire.

By now the sun was well down toward the horizon. And Uncle Joe began to feel some qualms about driving into the night. He felt too inexperienced with a motor car to consider traveling strange roads after dark. As he said, you could never tell about an automobile. It hadn't the sense of a horse that would take you home in spite of yourself. Fortunately he'd had the foresight to engage Otis Tarbutton for the farm chores, just in case they were delayed. So they'd best play it safe, pulling into a grassy woods path along the road and sleeping in the car. They spent a miserable night. There was no way they could get comfortable. With the curtains up, the heat was oppressive; curtains open, they were eaten alive by mosquitoes.

At crack of dawn they pulled out. It had been a long night. Uncle Joe said ruefully, "I dunno. Seems like we're born losers."

His sister refused to complain. "But, Joe, let's remember the fun." She gave Jay a poke in the ribs. "Didn't we have a swell time?"

"Yeh," he answered with a little crooked grin.

Their joy in the Ford was short-lived. It happened the one Saturday night of the entire summer that they decided to take in a picture show. Coming out late, they turned briskly down the shadowy street, in laughing colloquy about the fun parts of the show. When they reached their parking, gaiety turned to shock. The car was gone! Two buggies stood at the hitching rack, but down towards the far end where they had left the machine there was only empty space. Stunned, they just stood there.

Charley Tarbutton, whistling and stepping along right lively as he returned from seeing his girl to her home a block away, recognized them and wondered why they were huddled in the street, since a rig besides his own was waiting at the rack.

"Good evening. Is there trouble of some kind?" And when they told him, he too stood dumbfounded, his glance absently searching about. "But who on earth could have taken it?"

"I've no idea," Uncle Joe said wearily.

Charley still pondered. "Maybe it was an emergency, and you'll hear from somebody."

"It's possible," Uncle Joe agreed. "But it does look mighty peculiar."

"Well," Charley said finally, "it's awful late to do anything. Let me drive you folks home. Then first thing in the morning maybe we can find out something."

They crowded into his buggy, Jay jackknifed into the back as was his usual lot. Jogging out the road, Charley kept puzzling over the mystery. "Now who in the world could have taken it?"

"I wish I knew," Uncle Joe said.

They soon found out. The thief, an escaped convict fleeing police, had been killed and the car demolished by a speeding train.

That ended it. And Uncle Joe bemoaned their loss until his sister finally said, "Oh, stop your fretting. It could have been worse. One of us might have been killed. We got along quite nicely without it before. And we will again."

As Uncle Joe had pointed out, Mrs. Tarbutton really could claim part ownership in the camera, since she had refused payment for her coupons. And in return for her generosity, Jay delighted the family with snapshots of everybody.

Two of the older boys had rescued from neglect and abuse a big old black horse. And when he was somewhat restored to health, they were eager for his picture. Choosing a mild Sunday afternoon with cloudless blue sky, Jay and his mother drove over to Tarbutton's. What was to have been a simple bit of business turned out to be a major production. Besides the horse, a dog and cat were added to the "sitters," and various others among the farm animals lent their unwelcome presence.

DRAMATIS PERSONAE

Charley Brown .... Horse, black, old.

Sport .... Dog, wheaten Terrier.

Lulu .... Cat, orange tabby.

Sweet William & Nanny .... Goats.

Connie .... Cow.

Priscilla .... Sow.

Buckwheat .... Burro.

Such a time they had with Charley Brown! He might be twenty-eight years old but feminine allure still stirred him and superhuman restraints could not hold him still. When Charley Tarbutton rode him over from his pasture, mares in a nearby field brought him pounding up the road bugling every step of the way. And he was determined to pay his respects to them. Charley and Jay struggled to keep him beside the stone wall of the barn lot. He whinnied and stomped about, dragging on his halter rope until Jay barked his knuckles on the rough mortar between the stones. To keep the big brute occupied, a bucket of grain was brought and doled out by the handful.

Meanwhile, little Billy boy wanted his wheat-colored Sport dog in the picture. Then Elly fetched out her orange cat. Jay decided that these two on top of the wall with Charley horse looking over would make a fine picture. It was not to be.

Sport had rolled happily in the barnyard and got his hair full of straw and stuff. Lulu cat, lugged out from her cool siesta in the house, wanted no part of the proceedings. Elly, hiding behind the wall, tried to hold her in place, but Lulu laid back her ears with a snarl, and scratched herself free of the grasping hands. So, they would concentrate on just two: Charley horse was bribed with little dabs of grain, and good-natured Sport tried to be patient. But the sun beat down and he began to pant. If not held in place he would jump down off the wall.

Meanwhile, the commotion attracted several other animals and they all fore-gathered to observe the goings-on. The goats, Sweet William and Nanny, crossed a wide field from its furthest corner, Connie the heifer came thundering around the barn and slid to a stop on her knees, an enormous white sow espied the grain bucket and had to get right in the middle of the melee. One and all they did their best to spoil the day's masterpiece.

Owner and horse having the same given name, it became necessary for Jay's directorial bellowing to distinguish whom he was addressing—Charley-man handling the grain bucket, or Charley-horse nibbling the goodies. So it was—

"Charley! Charley-man, hold the bucket away from the wall. (Git! to the goats crowding him.) Here Charley, Charley-horse. (Hey. Shoo, pig!)" He was down on his knees trying for the best high level shot. ("Beat it!" the goats back again.) And the sow sniffing around nearly knocked him over.

Everybody working like beavers, with flailing of arms and lifting of boot, they spent a heroic half hour without getting much to show, perhaps one decent picture. Charley Tarbutton's clothes were a mess. Charley-horse slobbered all over Jay's clean shirt, one of the goats sneezed and splattered his good suit with snot, and he stepped in dung with his second best shoes.

From the barn's cool shade came the voice of Buckwheat, the burro, "Haw ee, haw, haw, haw."

While the onlookers laughed, Jay could see nothing funny about it. And driving home, Mrs. Malone had trouble keeping a straight face.

For Uncle Joe the Ford had been a welcome addition to their stable of vehicles. Jay was fast growing up, and the buggy could not comfortably accommodate the three of them all at once. They needed something roomier. Now, once more faced with the problem, what they should have, he decided, was a surrey. One that could be bought cheap. And towards the beginning of winter, opportunity knocked. Attending a farm sale when the weather turned foul, so that the crowd was sparse, he picked up a bargain, so well kept that it shone like new. They gave it to themselves at Christmas. Now, there was not only ample room for family, but they could also enjoy a guest.

Their first adventure took them on a Sunday drive to look at a boat. This was a lifeboat said to have washed ashore, probably from the sinking of some ocean liner. It carried no identification, so the story went, and its origin was never discovered. Uncle Joe, liking the idea of something unsinkable, thought he might buy it.

"How about a picnic?" his sister suggested. "And invite Captain Roth. We'll go right by his place. And the boat should interest an old sea dog like him."

A capital idea! So she mailed a little note of invitation. And on Sunday next they packed a large hamper of crispy fried chicken with all kinds of goodies.

The Captain awaited them, seated on his porch and joined by several lazy cats taking their ease. In jaunty cap and dark blue coat with brass buttons, lively as a cricket, he skipped down his walk, gave them a quick little salute, and climbed up beside Uncle Joe.

"Very interesting," he commented, hearing about the boat. That it was now all over painted gray seemed to him very odd indeed. "I would suspect that the fellow who found it lost no time in covering all telltale signs."

"Well," Uncle Joe said, "that happened quite a while back. He's dead and gone now. And there have been at least two other owners."

A wizened farmer with eyes the color of a goonie and sandpaper whiskers led them along his pier. Uncle Joe, Jay and the Captain took the boat out for a try. They liked its smooth rowing over the water and its buoyancy. The taciturn farmer silently watched them, standing by the seat Mrs. Malone found for herself while she waited. He was surely not a man to waste words.

A deal being struck, and the farmer agreeing to deliver the purchase, picnic was next on their minds. But before they had found a suitable spot, they drove through a heavy shower that drenched the countryside. Not to be denied, they decided to picnic in the carriage. Dewey being fastened to a line fence beside the road, Mrs. Malone opened the hamper and began supplying each one's portion.

But Uncle Joe hardly got started. As he was about to bite into his big juicy drumstick, something, they never knew what, startled Dewey, and the carriage lurched as he strained against the fence. Uncle Joe wildly grabbed the reins to calm him, and lost his drumstick. What happened to it, they never knew. It appeared to be nowhere in the road, nor along the ditch beside the carriage. It seemed to have disappeared into thin air.

That was a picnic they never forgot. And the case of the vanishing drumstick always made Capt. Roth's pot belly shake.

★ ★ ★

Chapter X

At the beginning of his senior year in high school, Jay awakened to the bliss of romance. He was smitten by a charming new girl named Louise Johnson. She had "raven" curls, big dark eyes and a ravishing smile. After noticing her for a day or two, he realized that some of the fellows, who were better looking than he, had begun to take notice. So he sent her a little note up along the aisle in study hall.

"Hi, Girlie. I think you have some eyes. What do you say to ice cream after school? Jay Malone."

She turned her head over her shoulder and nodded, "Yes."

He tried to send her another tightly folded note, but the teacher intercepted it and waggled her finger at him. For half an hour he was uneasy that she might read it. But when the bell rang, she handed it back, clucking her disapproval.

After lunch, as they passed in the hall, Louise winked at him.

Jay learned that she lived three miles out of town and drove in each day. Persuading his friend Gus to let him leave his bike at the livery stable, he had a good excuse to walk over with her each day, carrying her books and treating occasionally to ice cream or elegant pink and green confections from the Greek candy store. Winsome Louise made a picture emerging from the stable in her little parasoled buggy drawn by the sleek black pony at a brisk trot. Jay knew that he was not Louise's only beau, but his camera was immensely popular.

When it happened that they were assigned to the same side of a debate, Jay was thrilled to find an excuse to call on Louise in her home. He rode Dewey over Sunday afternoon. Her parents were away, but the place was swarming with children. It was difficult to do much work, but still they were together for a little while.

He and Louise went steady, more or less, for the whole year. Especially was she devoted at Christmas time when with his meager hoarded savings he bought her the manicure set she hinted for.

Jay graduated from high school, valedictorian of his class. And Uncle Joe, who valued education (his own classroom attendance ended with the eighth grade), was so proud that he had to be restrained sometimes from bragging too much.

That milestone passed, now what? The question was nagging for all of them. Each wondered, but nobody brought up the subject.

Uncle Joe well knew how much he depended upon Jay. Yet he was ambitious for the boy. Farming offered no career for a smart young man. And farm work needed a person physically strong; whereas Jay was not at all robust. But until asked, the old gent was not of a mind to offer his advice.

Mrs. Malone shrank from painful thoughts, dreading that inevitable day when her son would leave home. For the time-being, she was content just to let matters take their own course.

Jay gave some thought to attending college. But getting married was also on his mind. And for that he needed a job. His mother, suspecting his inclination, prayed that he would not do some foolish thing.

Following graduation came the summertime and considerable distance separating them. Louise was nearly six miles away. And Jay, despite his ardent longing, found it difficult to call on her as often as he wanted. They did write. But letters hardly sufficed. Although he had told her that he was planning on a job in Baltimore, that had not come about. Uncle Joe, not so young anymore and troubled with rheumatism, seemed always to be needing him. So that whether from pure bone weariness or simply lack of time, Jay found it hard to very often go courting.

But bigger troubles lay ahead. A Tarbutton uncle died suddenly, leaving his huge acreage to the two brothers. So they had to give up farming on shares for Uncle Joe. The outlook was grim. Jay knew where his place was.

That year the weather prevented very much Fall plowing, which would mean a busier springtime. Still, they mended fences, replacing rotted posts and tacking on new wire. When it was too wet or too cold for anything else, they might oil and polish the sets of harness. Uncle Joe, like his sister, was a meticulous housekeeper. And repairs were needed on the old buildings, fixing this and that or some other thing.

Towards noontime of a blossomy day in the early spring, Jay, dreaming of his Louise, rode home from town after standing around all morning waiting his turn at the blacksmith's. He found his uncle astraddle the ridgepole of the barn repairing a leak in the roof. Dismounting he called up, "Need help?"

"Nope." Uncle Joe hammered in the last nail, "I'm just finishing." Shifting his position to step down the ladder, he suddenly disappeared on the opposite side of the building. Fearful thumping and bumping panicked Jay. Dropping the saddle just unbuckled, he raced around the barn to where his uncle lay on the ground. Grimacing, Uncle Joe whispered, "I'm afraid I can't get up."

Jay gasped, "I'll run fetch Mom."

Between them they managed to ease the stricken man onto a heavy horseblanket, then ever so carefully they carried him to the house. When finally he lay on the couch in the kitchen, Mrs. Malone began applying such remedies as she knew. Jay resaddled Dewey and galloped back to town for the doctor.

Uncle Joe had severely sprained his back and broken his right leg. "Well," Dr. Blades said, "it could have been worse." Meaning Uncle Joe could have broken his neck. Luckily he had pitched down the gently sloping roof on the side where it joined the hog pen by the wagon shed, and his fall to grassy earth was not more than four feet.

But Uncle Joe considered the damage bad enough. Never seriously ill a day in his life, he was a rebellious invalid. All during his convalescence he fretted and fumed over his uselessness, sitting there day after day, with all the work to be done and him unable to pitch in.

In the weeks following, Jay found out what he was made of. Together he and his mother undertook to handle the farmwork.

Every morning they rose shortly after five o'clock, going right out to the barn to feed the stock. While the cows were eating, they milked. Jay brought the milk up to cool in the half barrel filled with water at the pump, while his mother let the cows into the barnyard, watered them and started the herd out to pasture. While the milk was cooling, they ate breakfast.

By eight-thirty Jay was out in the field. He would plow until he saw the white rag on the post. Unhitching, he brought the horses up and watered them, standing by lest they drink too fast or too much. Then he fed them. After dinner, as soon as the team had finished eating, he would go out again and stay all afternoon. And he thought, "What the hell does a farmer need rest for? He's got from ten at night till five in the morning." Dragging his weary frame through the evening chores, he ate supper and fell asleep in his chair.

His mother fed the hogs twice a day, and the chickens. She tended the garden. Every Monday was wash day, each Thursday she baked bread. Wednesday night she got her yeast ready; next morning when Jay came down there would be a big old doughtray on a couple of chairs and she'd be putting warm irons into one end.

Their routine was monotonous as a treadmill. Forever work, rarely pleasure. And though it was the lovely season when a young man's fancy turns to thoughts of calling on his girl, Jay barely made it every two weeks. So he was rather relieved to get a note from Louise announcing that she was leaving on a trip to Philadelphia for a visit with her aunt. She did not say how long she planned to be gone. But by the time she returned, Jay imagined, Uncle Joe ought to be back in harness, and he could find more free time. Thoughts of the pleasures they would share sweetened his drudgery.

★ ★ ★

Chapter XI

Jay was probably the last person to learn the truth about Louise: that she had gone not to Philadelphia visiting her aunt but to Atlantic City on her honey-moon. One of her gabby little brothers spilled the beans. And right in the middle of Main Street! Jay despaired—always the loser.

On a Sunday afternoon, home alone for an hour or so, he lolled in a porch chair agonizing over his broken heart. Josh nearby offering his sympathy pricked up his ears and growled. Then recognizing their friend Flossy McGuire, he dashed out to meet her just entering the lane.

Flossy and her mother were regular visitors down from Baltimore to spend several weeks at Price's Inn on the opposite side of the point. Although she was a sophisticated city girl of twenty-three engaged to marry a navy man, Flossie looked scarcely older than a pretty teenager. Small and dark, her black hair nightly curled on rags, her smile dimpling both cheeks, she was a lively personality. The fleeting expressions of her pert countenance intrigued Jay. It troubled him not at all that her nimble mind could out-distance his. They were pretty good friends. And his mother had become immensely fond of her.

He met Flossy soon after Prices built their rustic pavilion overlooking the water. There by the light of lanterns, to music from a Victrola, young people gathered to dance—those staying at the inn mingling with couples out from town. Jay was not of their class. Not only were the fellows older and very smooth, but the girls acted stuck up, humbling him with their icy stares.

Still, he enjoyed watching them dance and listening to the music. On a gentle slope near the pavilion stood a solid old wooden two-seater swing that provided a front row seat comfortable for him and Josh.

Then one evening the imp that was Flossy tripped lightly down the path and paused beside him. "Hello," she said with her dimpled smile. "You're not dancing?"

It embarrassed him to confess that he didn't know how.

She ignored his diffidence. "Then it's time you learned. Come on, I'll guide you." She took him by the hand.

He hung back. "But I'm not dressed."

"Neither am I." She pulled him toward the pavilion.

"You wait here," he told Josh.

In a dim corner they began the lesson. Beyond a wave of her hand in greeting, Flossie paid no attention to the dancers. Jay's sense of rhythm helped him to catch on rather quickly. Soon he forgot his shyness. Generous with her praises, Flossy urged him to come over whenever he could. And after a few visits he felt at ease so that he dared invite Louise.

For that evening everything must be just right. He had even calculated on moonrise. He groomed Dewey and polished the buggy. For himself a barbershop haircut and his carefully pressed good suit turned out a nice young man whom his mother and Uncle Joe looked upon with fond pride.

Neatly dressed, with a light heart he was on his way. But starting down their steep stairs he slipped and skidded the whole way to the bottom. His descent raked the top off a big boil on his behind that he had been determined to ignore. And worse, he sprained his ankle.

Uncle Joe turned coward at the thought of Jay's bitter disappointment. He said, "I'll quick ride over to Johnson's so Louise won't be wondering." And the good man made his escape.

Flossy commiserated with Jay then, and she tried to console him now. She had walked over to let him know that she and her mother were down for three weeks, and to show him the present from her fiancé. It was a gold link bracelet secured by a heart-shaped lock with miniature key. It had belonged to his mother who died, which seemed to her so sweet.

Finding Jay downcast, she tried to coax a smile. "Well, what's ailin' you?"

"Nothin".

"Don't tell me that. I'll bet you and Louise have had a fallin' out."

"Guess again," Jay said somberly.

She gave him a sharp glance but didn't ask.

"She's married," he said dully, staring away.

Flossy fell back in her chair. "Oh, I'm sorry." she said sincerely. For a moment she was silent, stroking the top of Josh's head. She looked at his unhappy face. "But if it's over and done, Jay, moping won't help."

"I know," he said. "And I guess it's better this way, to break up now rather than after we'd be married."

"Right," Flossie agreed. "You'd not want an unhappy wife." She laid her hand on his arm. "Louise was bound to see that it wouldn't work out."

"Why?"

"Well, she must have realized that your mother wasn't keen about you getting married." Flossy looked very young but she had an old head, and she was close friends with Mrs. Malone.

"Mom never was rude to her."

"No. But there are other ways of letting your feelings be known."

"I see what you mean. My mother never let me know how she felt about Louise. But Louise knew."

"Exactly."

"She might have suggested that I bring her out to the farm. She never did though."

"How often did you call on Louise?"

"About every two weeks."

"When?"

"Sunday afternoon."

"What an ardent admirer!" Flossy laughed merrily. "Every two weeks on Sunday afternoon. How long did you stay? And what did you do?"

"I won't tell you. You're laughing at me now. Anyhow, it's private."

"But if you only called on her every two weeks, did you go right after dinner and stay till bedtime, or was it a short couple of hours?"

"I'm not going to tell you."

"My admirers come on Sundays at two-thirty and stay till Mama runs them home about ten-thirty."

"I'm not interested in the calling hours of your admirers."

"Yes," Flossie said reflectively. "I can perfectly understand Louise's viewpoint. Here was a farmer boy who called on her maybe—notice I said maybe—every other Sunday. She looked out to the farm and what she saw was dismal: a cool reception from the in-laws and a life of hard work. Pretty as she is, you can't blame her for accepting somebody else, Jay."

"She knew that I was thinking about a job in Baltimore," he offered.

"You told her, but had you made any definite plans?"

"No. Not yet."

"Then she probably thought you couldn't be serious."

"She probably thought if I could go away to Baltimore and certainly be gone more than one Sunday in two weeks, then I could come to see her oftener."

"Naturally. You can't blame her, Jay. It's just too bad for you. I'd say you're a victim of circumstances."

"That's been my lot since the day I was born," he said miserably.

"What did you do when you called on Sundays?"

"Took walks."

"Walks?" A smile hovered about Flossy's lips.

"Yes," he answered with dignity. "We went out walking."

"I suppose there was too much family for you to sit peacefully at home." Flossy drew with her long fingernail a neat part in the fur on Josh's head. "How many brothers and sisters does Louise have?"

"One, two, three—seven at first count. But I'm sure there are more. They all belong to her stepmother. One of her little brothers took a great fancy to me. She'd say to him, 'I think Daddy wants you in the yard.' He'd say, 'I'll be back in a minute.'"

"Then I suppose when his little back was turned you and Louise moved together on the sofa."

"There wasn't any sofa. Nothin' but straight chairs."

"What a handicap!"

"The first time I visited her, two of her brothers were playing Parcheesi on the same table where we were working on a debate."

"Oh, so a debate brought you together?"

"No. We met at school."

"Did you ever take her to see a movie?"

"No."

"You never did? Did you take her some candy?"

"Yes, But not every Sunday."

"Did you ever surprise her with a tiny bouquet in the wintertime?"

"No. But I took her an apple once."

"An apple!" Flossy was convulsed. "What a naive beau. An apple!"

"Some girls appreciate an apple," Jay said huffily.

"I can imagine." Flossy's lips twitched. "Really, Jay, I don't know why she put up with you as long as she did. If she was like the girls I know, she would have said to herself, 'Why should I sit at home and entertain him? If he can't take me out, I won't be bothered.' And she would have jilted you without any qualms."

"Well," Jay said mournfully, "that's exactly what she did."

★ ★ ★

Chapter XII

His love lost, Jay's melancholy seemed perpetual. His mother and Uncle Joe worried about his lack of interest in anything.

Then one Saturday driving home from town he mulled over a new idea. On the street he had run into a former classmate who was enthusiastic about his government job in Washington. Life in the city was a lark. The pay was good and regular. You could mail-order the study material to prepare for the civil service exam. This, Jay thought, was the push he had been needing. Now be felt freer to leave, since two of the younger Tarbutton boys had approached Uncle Joe about farming on shares.

When he opened the lane gate, no Josh came bounding to welcome him. Out with Uncle Joe probably. But Uncle Joe was at the house. Jay called and whistled. No response. By supper time he bad become genuinely alarmed. Josh never missed a meal. Jay searched the barn and the boathouse. And up late into the evening, by moonlight, he crisscrossed the fields, peering into thickets. A dog could get caught in broken fence. He called Josh's name and repeated his special whistle which usually brought the dog from anywhere in hearing.

Through the night, unable to sleep, he worried, several times going down, praying to find Josh on the porch. And Sunday morning he looked hopefully for the eager face and waving tail. After milking he gulped a cup of coffee, then went to search the woods. Their timber was posted, but some sneak might have set a trap. From side to side, forth and back, methodically he pushed through the underbrush, calling, whistling, peering right and left, pausing to listen for his pal's answering bark.

When for the third time he came out onto the old sawmill road, his heart stopped. There in a heap lay the beautiful golden brown body. Josh had been shot. And he must have tried to crawl home. With a moan Jay collapsed beside him, cradling the lifeless dog in his arms, his grief hysterical. One cheek pressed against the broad furry brow, he kept repeating, "No! No! No!" Suddenly he raised his head and glared, his face contorted with rage. Was somebody watching him? He'd kill the bastard!

But there was nobody. Only himself, alone there in the whispering stillness of the deep woods.

In misery he stumbled home. His mother was shocked to silence at the look of him. Without a word he climbed the stairs to his room and came down carrying a quilt from his bed. He went out, slamming the door, and took his little red wagon from the shed.

The sight of him returning wrung Mrs. Malone's heart. In the ancient family burying ground out back of the house, Jay dug a grave and gently lowered his beloved friend wrapped in the quilt. Runners of Grave Privet greened the spot.

Jay was grief-stricken. Wherever he looked, there was the vision of Josh. Open the door, he could see his eager pal waiting. But there was only emptiness. At the lane gate where he was always welcomed home; there at the end of the pier sharing secrets; on the old leather couch napping together. . . Memories made him cry inside, silently. Regrets—that he had not paused to savor more deeply their beautiful friendship. Guilt—remembering when Josh outside his closed bedroom door had given a little bark asking to come in, and he had been too busy to answer. Then he heard the dog go slowly down the stairs. Now, if only he could relive that moment. He tried not to remember. Only time could dim the visions that haunted him.

Miserable as he was, he knew that he had to get away.

His order for the civil service study material brought an early reply. And such was his careful preparation that he made an excellent passing grade.

In due time he received a job offer—Clerk in the War Department. The irony of it! After all his dreams of a military career, to perform his war service in the file trenches!

★ ★ ★

Chapter XIII

Jay arrived in Washington towards the middle of June. He had expected to stay at the Y, at least temporarily, but it was full. The desk clerk directed him to a private home. There the landlady had available only a third floor hall bedroom, very narrow with one small window, but Jay immediately rented it for fifteen dollars a month and dropped his worn valise beside the bureau. His budget would be darn tight to begin with.

How tight he learned next morning. Though he had come on an offer of $1200 per annum, what he got was $1140, "Right stingy of Uncle Sam," he mused. Nevertheless, this was his opportunity and he would do his best. His dependably good work—he kept at it, and no cheating just stuffing the files in any old place—in time brought a commendation from his supervisor and a piddling raise.

But he was so very lonely. The big city offered less excitement than he had imagined. He knew nobody; his former classmate had moved on. And Jay was not the sort who make friends easily. The people he met remained mere speaking acquaintances. He saw the sights, wandered for hours through the museums, hung around the Ellipse watching any ball games in progress. Evenings he read the newspaper, then went to bed. Sunday mornings he dropped in at the services of the Methodist Church around the corner. The congregation greeted him in friendly fashion, but there seemed to be few young members. Only very rarely did he allow himself the luxury of a movie. Living so close to George Washington University, he considered it criminal not to pursue his education. And for a class or two come Fall, he had to save.

His landlady's aged father, crippled by a stroke, was somebody to talk to. In fine weather Mr. Shaw sat on a bench in front of the house where his friends in the neighborhood stopped to chat with him. But during the winter months he must remain cooped up in his room with only his green parrot for company. Jay got into the habit of sitting with the old gentleman, sharing a pipe of fragrant tobacco and playing cards or checkers.

Because he saved carefully, Jay felt in the spring that he could afford to be a bit generous with himself. On Sundays, when the less expensive government cafeteria was closed, he might treat himself to dinner at Allies Inn. It was pleasant while enjoying the delicious food to watch the pretty hostesses in quaint dress as they served coffee. And to avoid the long lines early, he went towards mid-afternoon when the crowds thinned out.

That Sunday, though it was mid-afternoon, with weather cold and damp, an unusual crowd filled the place. Jay had a small table for two all to himself only briefly when he heard a gentle voice:

"Is this place reserved?"

He looked up into the dark eyes of a young woman in pea green jacket and peaked cap with a curled green feather, holding her loaded tray.

"No," he answered, rising to help her.

"You don't mind if I sit here?"

"I'd be delighted."

For a grown young woman, her face and hands were remarkably small and pale. She had black straight hair cut short with bangs. When she unbuttoned her jacket and dropped it over the back of her chair, there was nothing to her. Jay had never seen such a tiny-tiny person.

Clearing her tray, she handed it to a waiter and began on her soup. They ate in silence.

Across the aisle from them, two women sat at table. One was large and bulky, with a mannish haircut. She wore severely man-tailored clothes and a pince-nez. Her companion, small and shriveled, was clothed in miscellaneous garments of rusty black with an enormous plum color hat skewered by a monstrous "jeweled" hat pin. She had a goiter, and her ear was stuffed with cotton. She talked continuously out the corner of her puckered mouth, chewing at the same time. Mostly she mumbled, but suddenly her voice rose above the din of the diners—

"Sure I remember Joey. We all thought he was dead, you know, after the war. But the Germans had took him prisoner. They walked him two hundred miles and gave him one loaf of bread. So when he come home naturally he was crazy.

"One day he says to me, 'I'm gettin' married.'

"I says, 'You gettin' married. Who you gonna marry?'

"He says, 'She's a girl that was gonna marry a sailor. But he didn't come back. The weddin' day's set and he ain't here. So I'm gonna marry her.'

"I says, 'What you want to marry her for? You don't know her, do you?'

"He says, 'No, I don't know her very well. I only just met her day before yesterday.'"

Her cackling laugh turned heads across the room.

Jay and the girl exchanged twinkles of amusement. After a moment of silence, he ventured a pleasantry. "I see you have something that I missed. What's under all that whipped cream?"

"Chocolate pudding." With her spoon she scraped off a little of the cream so that he might see. "And it's very good. I'd already decided on it when I saw a lady take some of this gorgeous chocolate cake, and I had to have some too. My sweet tooth is positively sinful." Her smile charmed him.

He wanted to prolong their chitchat. "Don't you find chocolate and chocolate rather too much of a good thing?"

"Well, yes," she admitted. "I'm certainly a poor judge of my capacity." Obviously she accepted her shortcomings philosophically. Certainly she had no weight problem; you could practically span her waist with your two hands.

From time to time her glance had wandered over the lively dining room, and now she found what she had sought. "I must go," she said. "Thanks for sharing your table." Gathering up her jacket, she crossed through the tables to meet an older woman just coming down the stairs.

Jay lingered with the lively crowd as long as he dared take up table space. With nothing to do, and nobody for company, he reluctantly walked back to his dreary room. The four walls seemed to close in on him and his window framed a dismal view. He was in no mood to study or write his weekly letter home. Lying across his bed, he tried to fall asleep so the hours would pass quickly.

Ten days later he discovered that the girl was also a University student. He caught sight of her entering one of the classrooms. Then in the library he found a vacant seat near her desk and smiled at her when she glanced up. Another time, as she tried to reach a high volume, he was there to hand it down. And he began to consider it a good omen that their paths should cross so frequently.

One evening passing the gym and hearing a lot of noise, he stepped inside. The girls' basketball team was holding practice. At once he saw her. From the side-lines she exhorted the players, shouting and waving her arms. Amused, Jay thought, "She's little but she's loud." And he watched her, fascinated.

Shortly afterward, from a distance he saw her fall on the library steps. Two young men were immediately beside her. And Jay felt a twinge of jealousy that he was too far away to help her up.

When he came upon her sitting on a bench in the Yard, with her arm in a sling, he dropped down beside her. "Did this happen when you fell the other evening? I saw you but I was too far away to lend a helping hand."

"No," she answered pleasantly. "I fell and broke my arm when I was trying to pinch hit for a friend at basketball practice."

Jay chided her. "Surely you know that basketball is not the sport for petite and delicate young ladies."

"I should have remembered," she agreed ruefully. "I'll never learn my capacity."

They both laughed. And it seemed to Jay that he detected a thaw in her reserve. She glanced at her watch. "I must get to class."

Though her charming image dwelt in Jay's thoughts, he was at a loss just how to warm up the acquaintance. Something special was needed. And he immediately thought of her when he was given a pair of theater tickets. They were pushed under his door with a note from one of the men in the house: "Jay. Hope you can use these. A friend sent them to me, but now I have to be out of town. V. W." They were orchestra seats for "No, No, Nanette" on Saturday night. The idea of escorting her thrilled him.

His strategy was to be on hand at her usual library study time, inconspicuously waiting so that it might seem they met accidentally. As it happened, she was a day late, but on Thursday evening she finally came. Jay emerged from the shadows to climb the steps beside her. As he held open the door, he said, "My name is Jay Malone. Can I invite you to the theater Saturday night? To see 'No, No, Nanette'."

A moment's hesitation, then she replied, "Sounds interesting."

Elated he hurried on. "Pick you up about seven?"

She dropped her books on a handy desk, found a scrap of paper and scribbled: Joy Hansen, 615 21st Street.

He liked her name. Joy suited her. And for two days he thought of little else besides their joyful evening. Friday his mind wandered from his work. Saturday the hours dragged even more slowly than usual. He dressed with great care. Though he'd never had the money to dress well, he was neat in his best blue suit saved for just such an occasion as this.

Jauntily he climbed the steps of the tan brick house numbered 615. When he asked for Miss Hansen, the elderly landlady ushered him into the parlor and told him to have a seat. He watched her go and pull a cord that hung down the stairwell. A bell jangled on high, and the cheery answering voice gave him a thrill. He heard quick footsteps along the upper hall, then down the stairs.

As he rose to greet his date, a perfectly strange girl appeared in the archway. She was a blonde, attractive, but too tall for Jay. Smiling, she said, "Hello."

Jay stared at her. "You're Joy Hansen?"

"Yes, I am." Her expression was friendly.

So he had been stood up! "Excuse me," he managed to say in a choked voice. "I'm afraid there's been a mistake." She was a party to this; she knew who had tricked him. And he wanted only to withdraw as gracefully as possible. "I'm very sorry to have troubled you." With a little bow, he turned and walked out.

Furious, he was tempted to drop the tickets in the gutter. Then he thought, "Why should I let her spoil my evening? The little bitch." So he went on down to the National and enjoyed the program, sitting beside an empty seat.

By the time he returned to his room, his hurt and anger had eased. Well, you could hardly blame her. He was no ladies' man. Disgusted, he studied himself in the mirror. Little peanut head, thin sandy hair high off his forehead, and a brown mustache old-fashioned as Uncle Joe's. What woman would want a puny guy half blind and gimpy besides? Hardly the figure for romance. You couldn't blame her. He was no Prince Charming. Just a born loser. And as a permanent reminder of his defeat he left the spare ticket tucked into the frame of his mirror.

Once afterward he had the misfortune to meet her. Unexpectedly they found themselves approaching each other along the Yard's central walkway. Her face changed. Jay gave her a little crooked smile and turned away on one of the side paths.

★ ★ ★

Chapter XIV

The departure of two third-floor boarders gave Jay what he had long wanted: a chance to move out of his cramped quarters and into one of the large bedrooms with big bay windows overlooking the G. W. campus. And he was especially pleased to be rooming with a young law student named Will Dawson with whom he already enjoyed a pleasant friendship.

One dismal Saturday during the midwinter holidays, their only mail was a small shocking-pink envelope with blue forget-me-nots across its flap and addressed to Jay in a precise round hand. But other than the "M" impressed in a blob of gold sealing wax, there was no clue to the sender.

Just returned from lunch, he dropped into their worn leather armchair, found his penknife and slit the blue blossoms to draw out a single pink sheet that brought a smile. "It's from a girl named Marta Williams," he announced. "She and I were kids together over on the eastern shore." His gaze rested on the dreary prospect of wet campus roofs under leaden sky. "I've often wondered whatever became of Marta."

She had written a very short note. He read it aloud: "Dear Jay—How nice that you're in Washington! I live here now. Right close to Union Station. Can't you drop by? Love, Marta."

Finding his pipe, Jay tapped the bowl against his shoe sole, tamped in rich tobacco, and touched a light to it. "It'll be really interesting to see Marta again. She was a lively one and very pretty. We used to play man and wife, and I'd build houses for her. She was always wanting to comb my hair." He chuckled. "I never could understand why women like to get their hands in your hair."

"It's one of life's pleasanter mysteries," Will declared with a crooked grin, gathering up his books on his way to the Libe.

Alone with his reminiscence, Jay hardly noticed the gloom gathering around him and the squally rain lashing the big windows. His fancy played in the sunshine of those happy days, a smiling memory of Marta's big brown eyes that sparkled with mischief. What a tease she was! He tried to picture her now, the attractive young lady, larksome still no doubt. And remembrance fueled a desire to see her again.

It would be amusing to recall what they were up to this time seven years ago: business partners sharing the proceeds from sale of Christmas trees at twenty-five cents each. What a woeful pair they must have looked, poor patched country kids trudging door to door taking orders. And how rich they felt sharing Marta's purse full of coins! Then skating on the pond in the woods— their antics gave Josh fits.

Seven years ago! And he hadn't been on skates since.

Rather than write, he would just surprise her.

Recalling their many shared interests, he more sensibly appreciated Marta's happy disposition and unselfish comradeship. He visualized her as about his height, naturally blonde, with pale complexion, sparkling dark eyes, and a quick smile. With her instincts for quality and her kind heart, she must by now be a very charming person. And through the days following her note, his thoughts dwelt more and more on the pleasure of renewing their friendship . . .

Her address was toward the middle of a long brick row on Capitol Hill. Stepping into the vestibule, he pushed the button of a raucous buzzer. A smothered voice answered, "Coming!" And he felt again that proper awe of Mrs. Williams. The door was opened by a small aged woman leaning on a single crutch.

"Miss Marta Williams lives here?" He studied her curiously.

She responded with a toothless smile and a nod.

This agreeable person could hardly be Mrs. Williams. She must be Grandmama. "I'm an old friend of Marta's," he said. "I dropped by to see her."

"Well, come in." She stepped back to open the door wider.

He entered a narrow, dimly lit hallway and followed her through dark-paneled sliding doors into the parlor. "Oh," she exclaimed, "let me go turn off the stove. Have a seat here, will you? I'll be right back." And she hobbled off down the hall.

Accepting the chair she offered, Jay looked about him. The dark-hued room too was dim, its crowded mahogany smothering the gleam of one small lamp. But from the shadows loomed an immense oil portrait of a woman in red. She was not young. Her figure had spread, her chin sagged, and marcelled graying hair swept back from her temples. But she was vividly made up and lavishly jeweled. Her lips were shaped in scarlet, her eyebrows had been thinly penciled. A heavy strand of turquoise beads filled in the low neckline of her red silk dress. Bulky blue earrings, an ornate brooch of varicolored stones, and two huge turquoise rings—all this composed a prodigal display. Yet she had encircled her uplifted arm with a gold chain bracelet dangling weighty charms. Her gaze was haughty, her presence overwhelming.

The crone had stumped back down the hall. "I'm so forgetful," she said. "But I promised I'd be ever so careful. Don't want a fire." She settled into a chair opposite. "Now."

"I was admiring the portrait," he lied.

"That's my daughter, Mrs. Williams. She was a great singer, you know. Wonderful voice. A very beautiful woman in her day." She sighed. "But for a number of years now she hasn't been at all well. After Mr. Williams died, it seemed best that we all live together."

"I came to see Marta," he reminded her.

"Oh, yes. Well, Marta isn't home. She and her mother are having their dinner down at the Mason House. I'm too slow walking that distance; so they carry out mine. They should be back soon."

Jay was disappointed. He had hoped to catch Marta alone, but to wait here was out of the question. "Perhaps I could meet them at the restaurant," he suggested.

"You might. The food is really quite good," she said pleasantly. "And it's not far. Only three blocks down toward the Capitol. It's right on the corner. Marta and her mother always go early and sit at the table next to the cashier's desk. Anyway, you'll see Mrs. Williams's red feather hat." She giggled.

"Then I'll walk down and join them." Rising, he held out the package he had brought. "May I leave this?"

"Why yes. Just put it down anywhere."

He placed his gaily be-ribboned box of chocolates on the small table just under the lamp, which made it the brightest object in the room.

The old lady ushered him out the door. "Marta will be glad to see you," she called as he turned jauntily down the sidewalk.

Immediately upon entering the restaurant he spotted the bright feather hat. Mrs. Williams sat against the wall; Marta had her back to the crowded room. But when he had gone through the cafeteria line, Jay decided to take a vacant table nearby.

One glance at the pair in the corner left him in shock!

Instead of the charming, vivacious young woman he had confidently expected, he saw a big overgrown girl with pale skin. Of age she might be, but without adult graces. There was a dismaying immaturity about her— in her set expression and, oddly, the cling of her blond hair at the nape of her neck, which reminded him of a Tarbutton infant daughter. Her clothes were kiddish and unbecoming: a homely crocheted hat of white wool, black-braided blue serge coat tight across the shoulders, and flat-heeled strapped black shoes.

On the second finger of her right hand she wore a cheap gold ring with a "ruby" set. Jay had given her that ring. They were poking through the moldering ruins of an old house partially burned and abandoned after a gruesome murder happened there, when he turned over a half-rotted plank and uncovered the ring. It was too big for Marta then, but she wrapped it with string for a snug fit. What a happy day that was, when they found the ring! Marta in a teasing mood kept playing tricks on him. Full of silly giggles, they walked home hand in hand.

And now. . . This was Marta? To believe it would make you want to cry. What could have happened? Where was the vivacious and charming little girl he had known?

Mrs. Williams's face was gray and haggard, with a bright spot of rouge on each cheek. She talked continuously, her voice droning on and on. Marta said nothing. Even when her mother seemed to be addressing her, there was no response, not so much as a little smile. The girl had a disturbing, unnatural quiet. Her movements were slow and deliberate, seeming to require the utmost concentration, as if she were dim-witted. She sat very still, eating slowly, mechanically. Though her eyes might occasionally rest upon her mother, their gaze was blank. Nor did she show the slightest interest in people around her. Beyond the thoughtful attention she gave her own simplest acts, her apathy was complete. The meal finished, she drained her tall glass of milk, tilting it high. Then she looked down into it and raised it again, licking the rim with the tip of her tongue. That done, she sat waiting, indifferent, remote.

Mrs. Williams's voice grew louder. She pawed through her old purse. Marta's absent air quickened not the slightest. Still rambling on, Mrs. Williams rose and fussed with her wraps, fastening close to her throat a ratty fur with dangling tails.

Marta got up slowly, heavily, and began buttoning her skimpy coat. Painstaking, like a child just learning, she fitted the buttons, each the size of a silver dollar, into their corresponding buttonholes. Having gone from top to bottom, she went back over them, using two fingers and pressing each button with a slight rocking motion.

Mrs. Williams accepted the brown paper bag just brought to their table, handed exact change to the cashier, and led the way out.

Marta followed, eyes straight ahead.

Stunned, Jay sat on, staring at the doorway that had swallowed them. Remembering the sprite she was, he wondered—would this zombie come to life greeting him? Her letter had seemed as natural as old time. What could have happened to her since they waved good-bye? He kept seeing Marta's face framed in the bull's-eye window and her little hand waving.

The thought of entering that house with those three women terrified him.

Three days later he sent a little note: "Dear Marta: So sorry I missed you when I dropped by. My time was shorter than I realized. But I'll be in touch with you. Love, Jay."

★ ★ ★

~

Chapter XV

His third summer in Washington, Jay scraped together sixty-eight dollars and bought an old jalopy he called "Nellie." It was a horror to look at, but it took him where he wanted to go, which was out into the nearby countryside. Old Mr. Shaw enjoyed going for a drive. So the two of them took Nellie up and down the river and out toward the mountains, bringing back peaches or apples bought at the orchards. On sultry summer evenings they might take a little drive to cool off.

During the next winter Mr. Shaw died. Jay missed the quiet game and pipe. He tried to cheer up the poll parrot. All the other roomers as well talked to the bird, now removed to the parlor bay window so that the old gentleman's room could be rented out.

For some time Jay had been thinking about a little place of his own. Something to busy him in his leisure hours. A home where his mother might come to live, should anything happen to Uncle Joe. With the blossoming of springtime he began cruising the streets of Arlington. Living in Virginia would be convenient to his office, and real estate was rather more reasonable out there. He had to find something cheap.

What he unexpectedly came upon was just about his style. For dilapidation it matched "Nellie." A traffic tie-up detoured him through a side street, and half way along there it was!

A weathered "For Sale" sign hung askew at the edge of the yard grown up in tall rank weeds. Beyond it, in a smother of foliage, loomed an old gray house. Jay pulled to the curb and sat staring at it. Obviously this had once been somebody's nice home. The building, left to ruin, was roomy, with double porches. Fine old oaks shaded the land.

What a pity the once handsome old house had been so sadly neglected. It stood wide open to the elements and vandals. Tattered, yellowed shades hung at broken windows. All the doors were ajar. Birds' nests clogged the rusted gutters. A fire had charred the rear wall above the kitchen. In the cellar around a rusty ancient furnace and an old-fashioned laundry tub with hand wringer attached, lay a waist-high pile of debris. Relics of vanished dwellers rose out of the chaos: an old wooden rocker, a low bookcase, some white cups and saucers on a rickety table, and music rolls from a player piano scattered over the earthen floor. On the wall shelves still held paint cans in orderly rows. How long since the laundry had been done here, or the paint cans were taken down for a little freshen-up job?

The "For Sale" sign carried a telephone number that put Jay in touch with the real estate agent. She told him the owners were wild to sell the place and would accept a rock-bottom price. To discuss it, he arranged to meet her there Sunday afternoon.

She was an overweight, over-eager gabby female. And not too bright, Jay thought. She began by telling him quite cheerfully, "It's called the haunted house."

"Why?" he asked, gazing up at the dumb facade.

She shrugged, perhaps afraid that she had said too much. "Oh, probably just the noises of wind and weather."

"Well, that's quite possible," Jay assented, "open like it is."

"Or maybe the former owners, wherever they may be, aren't happy with the indifference of their heirs," she added, trying to be clever.

"In that case," Jay said, "we might reasonably expect them to feel kindly toward anyone who cherishes it."

"I've heard there's a romantic story in its past," she rattled on.

"Romance only adds to its charm for me," he told her.

Then and there he mortgaged his future, wedded to restoring a dwelling in its decline. He knew that he had his work cut out for him, enough to last through years and years to come.

Restoration proceeded slowly, as Jay's time and funds permitted. Hardly had he been able to patch the worst scars so that the building was weather-tight, when Uncle Joe died. This meant that his mother would now come to live with him. Her letters had told how her brother's health failed before her very eyes. Heavy colds plagued him, and dizzy spells made him fearful. They thought something like that happened when he went out in the Clarabelle and failed to return. Otis Tarbutton found the empty boat and alongside, the old man's body snagged oddly in the anchor line.

Jay and his mother inherited the farm. They made sale of all but family belongings. And it seemed right that the Tarbutton boys were able to buy the land and stock, after they had pretty well managed the place since Uncle Joe got past working.

Though the house was anything but homey when she arrived, Mrs. Malone settled down with great pride in Jay's place. Never before had they enjoyed a home of their own, having always to rent or live in with others. She delighted in lending a hand toward beautification. She could hang wallpaper and paint woodwork. While Jay labored with hammer and nails, she kept the sewing machine humming. Her handiwork draped the windows and dressed the bedrooms. And under her green thumb, the yard blossomed with colorful flower borders. Favorite of hers were the Heavenly Blue Morning Glories that each year vined exuberantly over fancy wirework screening with beauty their porches, up and down. Looking for furniture, they frequented the busy auction houses downtown, afterwards disputing in amiable fashion just the right spot in the house for their latest finds. Once again Jay could enjoy companionship at home. He had hardly realized how much he missed his mother's good cooking. Together they settled into a comfortable quiet life.

When "Nellie" developed terminal disability of the rear end, Jay picked up a secondhand Chevy coupe which he painted light gray ornamented with red stripes across each door panel. He had a habit of referring to it as "the coffee pot." Now they could take trips up to Pennsylvania. Besides visiting with the few home-folks left, they liked to attend the farm sales.

A special drive up was called for when they learned that a sale would be held of effects from a family named Malone. (No kin that they knew of; way, way back maybe, but no recent connection.) The sale was already underway when they arrived and there was a goodly crowd. But they examined the glassware and dishes, prowled through the sets of old-timey furniture standing out in the yard. Then they joined the folks watching and waiting.

A bearded Amisher walked up. "Where's Catrine?" he asked. "She ain't out."

"She don't want to see her things sold," a voice answered.

Five fat old women sat in a row along the house wall, comfortably settled in the shade where they could keep track of and bid on items of the miscellaneous assortment piled on tables across the porch. Nearby stood odd little Miss Eby whose house full of old things Jay and his mother had visited. Thin, bent out of shape, dressed in an assortment of cheap, faded garments that were not too clean, wearing no stockings, her legs grimy and scratched, her strubbly "cheese and applebutter" hair escaping from under a small, shapeless hat, she paid strict attention to the selling.

Squatted in front of the five women and sitting on a basket was the penny man. He had big feet and big false teeth that he constantly gritted, and a good-natured idiotic grin. There was so much downright junk—saucepans you could see daylight through, jugs without handles, pitchers with snouts broken—that discards rained in upon him, rapidly filling his baskets. The auctioneer kept prodding him with penny purchases that nobody wanted. One box was already filled with trash, and he seemed puzzled over what he'd got, poking about in the clutter. A severe-faced old gentleman sitting nearby reached across and hooked the crooked handle of his cane over the edge of the box. The penny man grinned at him but kept a firm hold.

A simple-looking lad with dirty teeth laughed foolishly at every little bit of horseplay, his mouth glazed with spit.

The property was to be included in the sale. The auctioneer insisted that Mr. Malone built the house himself, and "it's built the way you like it— it has got wapor heat." In truth the building was crumbling, gingerbread trim in disarray and paint peeling. Its only charm was the sturdy trumpet vine in bloom that supported one corner of the porch.

The auctioneer held up a glass pitcher. "What am I offered for this nice little milk pitcher? It's got only one little bitty chip off the base, no crack up top. Who'll start the biddin' at one dollar? One dollar?" His glance roamed over the crowd. "Who'll gimme seventy-five cents? Seventy-five? Seventy-five? Fifty cents anybody? Twenty-five cents? Twenty-five?" He pulled from his hip pocket a blue bandanna and wiped his forehead. "Who'll have it fer nothin'?"

"I will," Mrs. Malone spoke up. In answer to Jay's quizzical smile, she defended herself, "Well, it's a Malone pitcher."

Jay bought for twenty cents a stack of linen napkins ironed and folded, commenting aside, "Hell, nobody ever wears out a napkin." But he made the mistake of unfolding one or two, and was chagrined to find them very much worn out. You could see his face through the holes in their centers. His mother teased, "Hell, nobody ever wears out a napkin." And people round about enjoyed the joke. Disgusted, Jay tossed the bundle into the penny man's basket.

Slowly the auctioneer inched his way toward an old shelf clock, grubby and abused, that Jay insisted spoke to him. Miss Eby took a notion to bid, but a dollar was her limit; so Jay got the piece for one-fifty.

Driving home they sympathized with poor Catrine, hiding so's not to see her things sold. "Poor woman," Mrs. Malone said, "outside her furniture, and even it was not all that great, she had a sorry lot of belongings."

Jay wondered that they hadn't thrown out the trash beforehand. "What do you suppose will happen to her now she's got nothing?"

After supper they took a look at their Malone family treasures. The quaint pitcher, on the dining table between them, was a jewel. Scrubbed of the cloudiness left by hard soap and over-used dishwater, the glass sparkled. Its pattern nearly equaled the intricacy of cut glass. Large clear ovals in relief were edged with beading of tiny glitter diamond points. In between were deep crosshatchings in small geometric designs. A scalloped band encircled the top, and on the handle a tiny sunburst provided the thumb-rest.

Mrs. Malone turned it about in her small pretty hands. "I'd be afraid to use it," she said. "Suppose it got broken. Besides being beautiful, it is eloquent of mysterious Malones."

"You wonder," Jay mused, "who bought it and what she looked like. Perhaps we should have talked with poor Catrine."

His mother still studied their find. "It should be just a shelf piece," she decided. "Set in place by a right-handed person—not left-handed like you— the chip would be hidden on the back side."

Jay grinned at her. "And where do you propose to show it off?"

"Oh," she replied airily, "I'll have to look around for the perfect spot."

And there was the clock. A humble timepiece, it was small and plain, with a pointed top, its face circled by large, black roman numerals, a rectangle of mirror hiding its pendulum. Its worn paint blistered and strips of veneer missing, it was a relic of hard times, likely over many years in some poor farm kitchen near the cook-stove, kept on a shelf with an oil lamp and a flyspecked calendar.

Opening the door on its front, Jay read aloud a printed sticker pasted inside: "8 day and 30 hour Gothic clock, one of the marine-lever timepieces for ships, steamboats, locomotives, and dwellings, made by Ansonia Brass & Copper Company, Ansonia, Conn." It was disappointing to find no date.

The clock's rusty striking was harsh and frantic—bang! bang! bang! But it didn't want to run. Jay made sure that it was wound, then nudged the brass pendulum. Several times, after two or three wags, it stopped.

"Needs a good dose of coal oil, I'll bet," he said. "From the looks, it never had any care. You know, it's kinda pathetic."

He went to collect his tools.

Meanwhile, Mrs. Malone dealt herself a hand of cards for a little game of solitaire.

Jay removed five small screws and lifted off a thin wood panel that completely closed the back. On the inside he found a notation written with pencil: "To Bill Malone for a Pig."

That gave them pause. Mrs. Malone sat holding in midair the card she had intended to lay down. They looked at each other. The story intrigued them. As Jay remarked, "Those few words raised questions thick as dandelions in springtime." Why had somebody felt it necessary to record the transaction inside the tightly screwed up case? Was there mistrust? What was the value? Where did this happen, and when? What were the people like? If only they could look back upon that little swap! In the past neither Jay nor his mother had given much thought to Malones beyond their immediate family. But these chattels, perhaps of their distant kin, casually happened upon, piqued their curiosity.

Jay said, "I told you it spoke to me."

★ ★ ★

~

Chapter XVI

For Jay the supreme event of a decade was the 75th Anniversary of the Battle of Gettysburg, which would be observed at the battle field with a final reunion of the Grand Army of the Republic and the United Confederate Veterans. Grampa Malone had been gone now some years, but here was one last chance to see and speak with surviving old soldiers, and to relive his boyhood hero worship, when he could still dream of military service.

He drove up to Gettysburg on Sunday, July 3rd, leaving home towards seven in the morning and arriving before nine. The air was cool after rain in the night, and at that early hour traffic was light.

On this day seventy-five years ago Pickett made his famous charge. The morning paper had recounted that tragic event. But Jay already knew the whole story. In his long preoccupation with military affairs he had thoroughly studied the Civil War. Poring over the pages of his wonderfully graphic history Blue and Gray, he learned the complete rosters of both armies and thrilled to the stirring descriptions of the various campaigns and battles. Pen portraits of the brilliant, dashing leaders, and reminiscences preserved, gave him a feeling of actual participation. His hero was Sheriden, "the war's most brilliant general," "the perfect warrior," reckless of his personal safety as he led his men... and "the earth trembled beneath the furious tread of his invincible legions of war steeds." He was brilliant, dashing, chevalious. Jay had dreamed of being such a man.

As he drove along, that day's action seventy-five years ago was vivid in his mind...

All morning both sides were busy making preparations. Then at 1 PM began their terrific artillery duel. The rows of 115 Confederate and 100 Federal cannon burst on the silence with hideous fire and roar. And for one and a half hours the air was filled with the continuous, deafening thunder of the big guns "hurling their bursting bolts of death." The earth shook. Fences, trees, rocks were blown to bits. A pall of smoke darkened the sky.

Into this fearful storm of leaden hail, half an hour after the bombardment began, charged the Confederate infantry, 15,000 strong. Eyewitnesses described Pickett's charge as like a dress parade; never was there a more gallant sight. In formation the column of assault pressed forward under heavy fire across the mile-wide open plain, into the bloody angle, their faces gaunt, their bayonets fixed. Shot and shell from the federal batteries tore great gaps in the advancing line. Each time, they closed ranks and moved on, unflinching. More than four thousand men in gray and nearly three thousand in blue fell within a few minutes.

But the desperate courage and appalling sacrifice was to no avail. Lee's brave men were repulsed. And of the magnificent column that had been launched so proudly, only a broken fragment returned. Pickett's charge was considered the climax of the engagement at Gettysburg, itself called "one of history's greatest battles."

A reenactment of the charge had been considered for this anniversary. But the plan was opposed on grounds that it might engender bitterness.

Probably today the countryside looked very much as it appeared before the three-day battle began. On the one hand stretched young green corn, knee high just as when the fighting trampled it into the ground. On the other, there was wheat in shocks. Lilies and hollyhocks were blooming. And tenting now on the old camp ground at the edge of the battle field were several thousand veterans—men mostly in their nineties, but some past the century mark. Today crowds of people from near and far would fulfill their country's "eternal honor upon its sons who gave their best, both victor and vanquished, in that war of brothers and neighbors."

Parking just two blocks from the encampment, Jay strolled along the boardwalks of the tent city. As he passed, old soldiers sitting in the shade of their tents greeted him with a smile and a salute. Some of the old fellows moved about in a daze, but many others were remarkably spry and alert for all their advanced years. Visitors shouted questions at them and they responded with ready answers. One aged officer quaveringly tooted his flute, to the enjoyment of a small crowd gathered. Another, hearing band music, executed a little jig with his stiff old legs. The courtesy and friendliness of the visitors was heartwarming. Everyone admired the veterans, and they responded with quaint little mannerisms in individual ways to the sincere homage.

The first veteran Jay met in the Union camp happened to be a visiting Confederate. He was a bent little old man in soiled and wrinkled gray, his coat sagging open, his pants legs rolled up, his shoes rusty. That uniform badly needed loving hands at home. Ninety years old, he had fought with the 36th Georgia Battalion. He said little, absently wandering around with his son in tow.

But in fine form was a veteran from Iowa who had been a sailor. His long gray hair curled up under the brim of this black hat with gold cord and GAR encircled by gold leaves. His white vest and the medals on his blue coat were dressy. He invited Jay to have a chair and rest a bit.

Though 92, he felt wonderfully well, except that he was rheumatic in the lower limbs. "So many of the comrades have rheumatism," he said. With suppressed eagerness Jay asked questions. The veteran sailor had served under Porter south on the Mississippi from Cairo to the Gulf as bosun's mate; that is, he was the petty officer on the gun deck who gave the orders.

He told Jay that his father and four brothers fought for the Union; his four uncles and their families fought for the Confederacy. "After the war," he said, "I made friends with the males, but the women never would see me. They felt their losses more than the men did. They never forgave Lincoln."

When Jay asked what he considered his most memorable experience, he answered, "I couldn't tell you." And gazing absently away, he repeated, "I couldn't tell you."

Next Jay stopped to visit with a fellow Pennsylvanian who was a telegrapher and received the word that Fort Sumter had been fired upon. What had impressed the young man was the wave of patriotism that spread over the north. He had been at Gettysburg, he said, "high private in the rear rank."

Oldest of all those Jay happened upon was another Pennsylvanian, 100 years and 9 months old, who had served in the 140th Pennsylvania Infantry under General Hancock. The poor old gentleman was peevish with fatigue. When his attendant sought to turn him around, he fussed, "Let me alone. Don't pull me about. Quit pushing me. I'm hunting the carpenter shop to get me some wooden legs." He had faced Pickett's charge. They marched all night and went into battle without any breakfast. But he was not wounded until the Wilderness.

As Jay was about to cross over to the Confederate camp, he met on the boardwalk two smiling veterans, one plump, the other lean, resplendent in fresh gray uniforms. Ninety-two and ninety-three, they had served with the 19th Tennessee cavalry. Jay marveled at their vigor. He said to them, "Your uniforms held up wonderfully well."

They chuckled. The senior comrade replied, "We just had 'em made three weeks ago."

And now, entertaining a crowd, here was an ebullient showman from the Southland who had served with the 16th South Carolina Regiment under Ben Goodley. He was 96, but acted younger than many men half his age.

"Do you feel 96?" He was asked.

"No. Only about 18," he replied. "I have a good time wherever I go. I'm full of anecdotes. A good laugh is better than medicine."

Below the brim of this black hat his white hair curled to shoulder length. He said, "I let the girls feel of my hair and beard. But the men? Never!"

A young woman lifted a curl to test him. He was telling one of his anecdotes. "A lady I let feel of my beard one day said, 'That don't feel like hair.' I said, 'It ain't hair.' 'Well, then,' she says, 'what is it?' I says, 'It's whiskers. And if you'll look close, there's two to a hill.' She says, 'Yes, there's two in each hole all right.'"

His audience laughed; so he went on. "I ain't married, but I've been lookin' around." He let his glance wander over the crowd before him. They waited, half smiling, for his next disclosure. He said, "In my time I've made peach and apple brandy and ten thousand gallons of liquor—enough to swim a horse from here to yonder."

"Did you drink it all?" piped up a bright-eyed youngster.

"No!" he thundered. "But," he added sweetly, "a little nip makes the ladies look so pretty."

After the war, when he came up for a pension, they asked whether he had ever been wounded. "No," he told them. "I never was mortally wounded. But I've been mortally scared."

"What do you remember best?" an admirer asked.

He grinned. "The running I did mostly."

Charmed by the old soldiers, his camera full of pictures, Jay was surprised that almost four hours had slipped by. Now that the tremendous crowds made quiet visiting impossible, it was time to leave. Though only one o'clock, the throng was estimated at 150,000, and all the roads were clogged with arriving cars.

But leaving was easy. And as he drove along, Jay reflected that he had heard no more talk of combat exploits from these old soldiers than he had from Grampa Malone. Nobody reminisced about the actual carnage. As one ninety-five year old Confederate veteran put it:

"The man who talks most about a battle was a long ways back. A man right in the fightin' don't have time to look here and there. He only loads and shoots."

★ ★ ★

Chapter XVII

Three days after Pearl Harbor, tragedy overwhelmed Jay.

Arriving home from the office he called his usual cheery, "Yoo, hoo!" as he closed the street door. But tonight there was no warm response. Puzzled, he looked about. Everything appeared ready to just warm the food and sit down to supper, except, where was his mother? This was so unlike her. She never failed to be there. It was her pleasure, she said, always to welcome him home.

About to glance over the house, he suddenly remembered that she had spoken of a trip to Alexandria with her sewing circle friends. This must be the day. But she had expected to be home in good time. No doubt she'd come soon. As he sat down to wait, the telephone rang. It was the hospital calling. Would he please come? Mrs. Malone had been in an auto accident.

Jay hardly knew what he was doing, speeding to the hospital, in a panic. It was even worse than he had feared. His mother was dead. Killed instantly in a freak accident. A truck out of control had collided with the car in which the five ladies were riding. Impact occurred just where Mrs. Malone was sitting, and she received a sharp blow to the head. None of her friends was seriously injured.

Grief-stricken, numb, Jay went about the necessary arrangements. He made sure that she wore her favorite rose silk dress with the brooch of pearls he had given her. When he found fault with the way her hair was done, the undertaker suggested that he might like to dress it himself. Combing a little more fullness about her face and coiling her long black tresses in a neat bun on the top of her head, as she always wore it, made her pretty face more lifelike.

And he must take her home to Pennsylvania; she would want to be laid away amongst family. But his return to the old home town was a painful experience. Nothing turned out as he had hoped. So few older Malones were left. And the younger generation, growing up, had responded to the lure of big city jobs. Even the kindly minister, whom Jay remembered fondly, despite his youthful distaste for attending church, had answered the call of a distant, larger congregation. The manner of his successor, Rev. Frost, was less warm, and a great disappointment to Jay. And he was a stranger. Besides, the weather turned wintry; between dark skies and sere earth, the still air was raw, with the hint of snow. The brave little cluster of kindly souls who had come to the cemetery stood bundled up, with their shoulders hunched against the chill. The faded flags hung limp and listless over the veterans' graves. Against the dismal scene Jay saw again the flower-scented sunny day when the crowd of friends and family stood waiting, and he proudly marched like a soldier.

Nature's gloom on this particular day hurt him. His thoughts about summed it up: cold sky, cold earth, and a preacher named Frost!

Back home, life hardly seemed worth living. He dreaded the long winter evenings, hating to turn his key in the lock. The big house was so empty and still. His loneliness enveloped him, there was a cloud over his days. Only his little Gothic clock had any life. Why was he such a born loser?

For a little company at mealtime, he got into the habit of eating his suppers at a small restaurant just three short blocks from home. The place occupied a charming old house once owned by wealthy people, so that the rooms were spacious with high ceilings, tall windows and working fireplaces. The chairs were comfortable, the tables not too crowded, and service was provided by attractive, sociable waitresses. During the dark days of winter Jay found some comfort there. He sat at the same table every night, and was waited upon by a pert young woman named Millie whom he liked to jolly.

One gloomy Saturday in March, feeling more than ordinarily depressed, he dropped by for lunch. Though it was still early, two other diners, a young couple, were already there, sitting just in front of him.

Three minutes before the hour serving was to begin, Millie entered the dining room. In her hand she held her stiffly starched little white apron, and as she listened to gossip from another waitress she tied it on. But not like the others did she catch it around her waist. Quite the contrary. Very particularly she placed the apron on front to back, and over her stomach she tied a great stiff bow in the wide strings. Her glance flitting from the face of her friend to the work of her hands, she measured the strings and formed a perfect big standing bow. That done, she twisted the apron around and smoothed its small circle down over her full skirt of gay flowered cotton. Jay got such a kick out of watching her.

Outside the sky was stormy. More rain threatened. Against a high wall great mounds of boxwood stood somberly dark. The young couple occupied a table beside one of the tall windows that admitted cold gray light, but their small table lamp gave their faces a lovely glow. An atmosphere of warmth and happiness surrounded them. They conversed in low tones, with eyes only for each other. He regarded her with adoring attention; she caressed him with smiling glances.

A banjo clock just visible in the hall chimed eleven. Millie edged away from her chatty friend, placed two glasses of water on a tray, and came to take the couple's order.

Though the menu indicated ham, there was no ham, because of rationing. Eggs there were, yes, and perhaps some bacon. The waffles were very good though they might want butter. The young pair, having had nothing to eat earlier, decided to combine breakfast and lunch. They agreed upon waffles with maple syrup, bacon (if any), scrambled eggs and coffee. Millie, waiting with pencil poised above her order pad, listened, then wrote down these items after verifying each one, and noting very particularly how the eggs must be scrambled not too firm. She had scarcely turned her back before the young people, sipping from their glasses of water, became once more absorbed in each other.

Coming for Jay's order, she gave them a smiling sideways glance with a little shrug. Millie was attractive and saucy at times. Jay enjoyed chitchat with her. She had told him that she was an only child, her father died years ago, and her mother clerked in a downtown department store. He liked her immensely. But he had seen her after hours hanging onto the arm of a husky, handsome guy in uniform.

Usually Jay lingered as long as he dared. Then when the room began to fill up, he settled his bill and closed the door on the animated crowd. Today, as he reached the wet sidewalk, he found himself looking into the wistful dark eyes of a handsome German Shepherd. The dog seemed to be lost.

"Hello," Jay said. "Where do you live?"

There was a slight wag of the tail in response.

Wondering how far he dared count on friendliness, Jay extended his hand. The dog touched it with the tip of his nose, remaining perfectly quiet.

"Will you let me read your tag?" Jay asked. Out the corner of his eye he could see the next intersection where five streets converged heavy traffic that could be murder for an animal. He had to get this fine fellow safely home.

"Yes," answered the tip of the tail, and its owner stood still while Jay twisted the collar around to read his ID. The address was somewhere up back of his place, he thought, though he couldn't be sure. "Come on," he said. "Show me where you live."

Obediently the dog turned and led him in the direction of home. The Malone house backed against a wooded hill down which dipped a rutted road, long unused, and it was up this way that the dog took him. "Hey! Wait for me!" Jay called as he fell behind, stumbling across the washouts filled with loose stones. The dog kept looking back, pausing while his rescuer caught up, then moving slowly on. Over the brow of the hill they came to a dirty white house where the street number hung upside on on the door frame. As they approached, there emerged a big beefy man with close crew cut and a dangling toothpick between his teeth. He looked at them without speaking.

At sight of him the dog stopped in his tracks.

Jay said, "I've persuaded your pet to come home. I was afraid he'd be killed in traffic."

"You want a dog?" the man asked abruptly. "You can have him. He ain't liked stayin' around since my daughter left. And I'm too busy to go huntin' fer 'im."

Jay looked down into wistful dark eyes looking up.

"He's a good dog, I guess," the man continued. "Anyways, my daughter paid a-plenty fer 'im. Don't ask me why. He's a dumb damn mutt. But now she's went to New York fer a job where she's got no room fer 'im. And he ain't been the same since she left. I was thinkin' mebbe I'd take him out in the country some'eres and dump him alongside the road. I ain't got the time to be no dog nurse."

Red hot anger flashed through Jay. But he said quietly, "I'll be glad to have him. Thanks."

"Wait," the man said, "and I'll get you his things." He went back inside, slamming the door. Jay stroked the dog's head, smiling down at him. And the tip of the tail responded.

When the man returned with a brown bag and a stout leash, Jay went forward to accept them. The dog did not move.

"He's got papers some'eres," the man said, "But I've no idee what my daughter done with 'em."

"Oh, I don't need them," Jay replied as he and his new found friend turned away. He hooked on the leash because he had decided, rather than negotiate the abandoned road, to go around the block. But the dog needed no control. He went along willingly.

Unlocking his door, Jay said, "Come in." And his guest politely entered.

Two bowls; pulled from the brown bag were filthy. Jay quickly washed and scalded them, filling one with fresh water. The dog lapped thirstily. He probably was hungry too. A little bite would stay him till his regular supper time. Jay offered some canned food from an unopened tin among his friend's "things." Three gulps and it vanished.

Having a pipe in his easy chair by the dining room bay window, Jay pondered this unexpected turn of events. The dog at first sat close by, studying his face. But invited to do so, he hopped up and lay on the cushioned window-seat. Jay wondered how anyone, even the stupidest, could give up such a handsome animal. His coat was so lustrous, his expression so intelligent. You got the impression that he understood every spoken word.

The dog must have a name but Jay hadn't thought to ask about it. He'd have changed it anyway. Breeders usually favor such ridiculous monikers.

"Well, now he's a Malone," Jay thought, "and probably the only family I'll ever have. Maybe I should christen him J. J. IV. Jack for short." The dog was watching him. "Jack?" he said, "Do you like that?"

"Yes," answered the responsive tail.

His ID should be changed. Jay went to find the pliers, and Jack followed along. Then they got busy putting together a suitable bunk bed in a snug corner of the bedroom. When supper time came, rather than slip down to the restaurant where Jack would not be welcome, Jay cooked a meal for himself and concocted for his companion something tastier than the usual dog food.

They spent a blissful evening, just the two of them. Rain poured outside, but indoors they enjoyed cozy companionship. Jay could hardly believe his rare good fortune. It occurred to him that he had given the man no information about himself. For that he was glad. Fickle daughter might change her mind about her job, might have other ideas about her pet. And from here on, nothing could persuade him to part with his treasure.

★ ★ ★

Chapter XVIII

So began their devoted comradeship. From the beginning, neither wanted the other out of his sight. When their first weekend passed all too quickly, Jay took a short leave. Contentedly puttering about, catching up on chores he'd not had the heart for, he talked to Jack, always close by. And they took long walks together beside the quiet branch in the woods of the nearby park. This mini-vacation brought Jay comfort he had not known lately.

But a man must earn a living. Inevitably, Monday morning came again, and with it, parting. Jay took the big dog's head between his hands and told him, "You look after things till I get back," then forced himself to close the street door. At the turn of this key that evening, Jack was ecstatic. He tried his best to talk.

Theirs was a joyful springtime. While Jay worked at this gardening or sprucing up their dwelling, Jack lay on the lawn observing the activity in their street. He made friends with the passersby: grown-ups walking down from the bus stop, youngsters going to or from school. The dog loved people.

And the kids, especially, thought he was wonderful. Jack knew what time to expect them and he usually stood at the front gate watching. If they stopped in, he willingly romped with them, chasing a ball, or retrieving any stick they threw. He was one of them. When a little girl in pink sweater and hair ribbons stooped to smell a pretty posy, Jack trotted over to have a sniff too. They could do anything with him. Once Jay happened to glance out the window in time to see a very small boy slap Jack in the face, then stamp on his toes. The dog only yawned.

Jack's earliest conquest was a black-headed, robust lad called Butch. He came down the street gnawing on an apple and paused to peer into the gutter, twisting his neck to read a sheet of water-soaked funnies plastered down with the sodden brown leaves. Glancing up, he became aware that he was being watched. There stood Jack inside the gate left ajar. A moment of wariness, then the boy ventured a "Hi!" And Jack responded sociably. Jay, up painting a porch post, called, "Don't be afraid. He won't hurt you." Butch crossed the sidewalk. "He loves company," Jay added, stepping down the ladder. "He'd be delighted to have you come, if you can spare the time."

The charmer in pink sweater and hair ribbon was Butch's baby sister, with the lovely name Aurora. Her mother and she walked over one Sunday to meet this fascinating character named Jack. Jay coming around the house was surprised to find them standing on the shade-dappled front walk. "Your garden is perfectly beautiful," she said.

Jay smiled, with a little nod and glance around.

She was a young, attractive, lightly-freckled redhead, wearing glasses, and her dress was of some soft material in pale frosted green. "I'm Catherine Warren, Butch's mother."

Jay knew that she was a war widow, and his sympathies embraced her. Butch had said, "My Dad died in the war." And Jay answered, "So did mine, nearly twenty-five years ago." With a wave of his hand he indicated his rustic bench. "I'm very pleased to meet you. Won't you have a seat?"

"I'm afraid we can't stay but a moment," she said. "Working mothers have many weekend home duties impossible to shirk. But I wanted to meet your wonderful dog—he has a five-star reputation—and to make sure that Butch doesn't annoy you. He's a great admirer of yours."

Jay shook his head. "No, indeed. Believe me, I'm having a ball."

She reached out to Jack and he offered his paw. She laughed. "Now who could resist such a greeting?"

Aurora had let go of her mother's fingers and toddled over to the nearest flower bed. Jack cocked an eye in her direction, then followed, to share in the perfume of a pretty blossom. "Don't pick, Hon," Mrs. Warren called.

Jay said, "Oh, let's give her a little bouquet. And you, since you haven't time to visit, must accept some roses to enjoy at home." For Aurora he cut three dainty single roses, each no larger than a twenty-five cent piece, pearly pink and richly fragrant, and carefully peeled off their thorns. "My mother was the gardener. She had a remarkable green thumb. But one of her whims I never could understand. Somebody gave her an unusual white rose, a gorgeous creation, beautiful to look at, but it had no more perfume than a tallow candle." For Mrs. Warren he was clipping long-stemmed perfect buds, rich red with heavenly fragrance.

Jack's circle of acquaintances among the younger set had grown. Butch introduced his buddies, Bill and Phil, the twins, and from time to time brought other friends. The kids all lived in tight little homes with hardly any yards to speak of, so that Jay's woods hollow offered the perfect gathering place. They whooped through episodes of cowboys and Indians, staged elaborate battles.

After a while there was Hallie, a lonesome little hanger-on. Tow-headed and tacky, she reminded Jay of the youngest Willey he had tormented so unmercifully. (What a stinker he was to tease her so, poor kid.) He was kinder to Hallie. So pathetically homely, a skinny child with lank hair, pale eyes and crooked teeth, she was still too young to realize the curse of her ugliness. She was an eager tomboy, but the fellows, noisily engaged in their private games, tolerated her only after Jay described the war exploits of brave Molly Pitcher.

It seemed that even then they tolerated her only because they could impose on her their dirty work. But Hallie was idiotically happy.

One of her playthings was a short length of sashcord which she liked to twirl for Jack to jump at. If he caught the rope between his teeth, they had a tug-of-war. He growled fiercely, she chuckled and shouted with laughter. Hallie adored the dog. And it made no difference to him that she was ugly as a mud fence. When next Valentine's Day rolled around, she left in the mailbox an "original" Valentine addressed to Jack Malone.

The coupe replaced by a sedan, several times during the summer Jay took a car full to the amusement park. Catherine Warren with Aurora shared the front seat. And though it was a bit snug for three kids and a dog in the back, they happily managed. Everybody, including Jack, had a barrel of fun riding the merry-go-round.

That was a year of pure happiness for Jay. He and Jack were inseparable. And they gathered around themselves quite a nice little family of other people's lively youngsters.

In October, Jay accepted an invitation to Tarbutton's big family reunion. It was good to see the boys again, and Mrs. Tarbutton's flushed face beamed on him as fondly as on one of her own numerous brood. The food was delicious, the friendliness and gaiety heartwarming. And Jay's snapshots of nearly everybody would fill a nice fat album.

While there, he meant to revisit the old haunts. Driving out to Uncle Joe's place his recollections unfolded like scenes in a motion picture. That familiar road—the many miles he'd traveled over it would likely have taken him half way around the world, and back. Five miles a day, twenty-five a week, and hundred a month just to and from school, not to mention numerous trips—walking, riding, driving—on other necessary business. Just imagine! And how much had happened since that first night when they rolled along in the hearse through the stretch of black-dark woods where foxfire glowed weirdly!

His mother had been petrified coming home late with their neighbor-lady. They were in the buggy behind her poky old horse. Midway through the stygian tunnel in close-pressing trees, where you could hardly see your hand before your face. Mrs. Davis said, joking, "Did I ever tell you about the bride who was murdered on the lonely road?" Mrs. Malone said, "Shut up!" What a relief when they finally turned out under open sky. They laughed about it afterward.

Just here he slid down Dewey's roached mane when the big Collie suddenly stepped out of the woods. And now the roof was collapsed on the ruined log house. How he had worried over Santa's plight in case the old fellow had gotten stuck down the chimney! Arriving once more at the lane gate, Jay could see again his beloved Josh, so eager to escort them up to the tall, mustard-color farmhouse, dark and silent in the embrace of giant trees.

In town, too, Jay had a mind to relive the past. Nosing in among the parked cars at the old hitching rack, he and Jack walked along the quiet street between the Episcopal Church and the jailhouse where the littlest Willey had permanently disabled him. They arrived at the school just as a bell sounded for the end of recess. From noisy revelry the square suddenly became silent. Time had brought changes. The big privies out back were gone; indoor plumbing had put an end to time-honored customs. In Jay's time the kids of the primary school considered it "the thing" to burst out of doors and race down the path to the privies, yelling, "Save a hole for me!"

On the harbor, a man working over his boat mentioned that the Ferry family had sold their big farm, and the fine old mansion was now an inn. Aha!" Jay thought. "That's where I'll spend the night." Imagine! Him sleeping in one of those elegant rooms! Him, a poor country boy never in the same class with the moneyed Ferrys. Their boys were older, of course, but he had envied their gay yachting crowd. The nearest he ever got to any Ferry was casual friendship with the hired man's kids.

Back at the parking he had just slipped behind the wheel when a sleek blue sedan pulled up alongside. Out of it stepped a plumpish, pretty, well-dressed woman. And he recognized Louise! As she faced Jay, her eyes betrayed recognition, but there was no change in her expression. Slamming the door, she walked away.

With a shrug, but touched by poignant memory, he backed out and drove over to the Ferry Farm. With secret excitement he climbed the front steps and eagerly entered the wide hallway. Everything—the floors, the furniture— was so beautifully polished, such elegant rugs lay before him, and against one wall a handsome grandfather clock ticked solemnly.

To the pale young man behind the desk, Jay offered his apologies for the lack of a reservation, explaining that he only just learned of the inn a half hour ago. Fortunately they had a room. But before he could sign in, the clerk caught sight of Jack waiting in the car. "You have a dog? I'm sorry. Dogs are not allowed."

Jay had practiced guile before. "He's my seeing-eye dog for night blindness." he explained. "If my one good eye fails me, as it sometimes does, I must rely on him. He's widely traveled. I assure you he has elegant manners and won't cause the least problem."

"Well." the clerk was doubtful. "But understand, dogs are not permitted in the dining room."

"Of course. Only on his personal blanket in my room."

Jay dressed for dinner. He found the dining room most attractive and the food delicious. If only his mother could have shared it with him. What a treat for her! It would have been nice to invite Louise...

In the evening he and Jack walked down to sit on the pier while he smoked his pipe and watched the big full moon rise over the river. It reminded him of his careful planning and happy anticipation of escorting Louise to the dance by moonlight on Price's pavilion. And then wouldn't you know, he had to slide down their steep stairs on his boil. Bad luck was his lot in life.

Except when he found dear old Jack.

Now he realized that it was well Louise had taken their future into her own hands. They were not meant for each other, as he then fondly imagined. He would have had trouble with her. Still, the dream was sweet while it lasted.

All night long quiet enfolded the house. Sleep was dreamy. And he awakened to a cool morning perfectly still. The mirror surface of the river reflected a wooded point opposite with its old gray house and short pier. Two ducks paddled about. Soon the rose-gold ball of the sun lifted above the far horizon and shot a sparkling path toward Jay's feet. No one else was up to enjoy this lovely scene. And Jay wondered how often the Ferrys had paused to appreciate it. So many of life's pleasures crowded their days, had they ever taken the time to drink in this beauty at their very door?

His enjoyable trip roundabout brought Jay and Jack home again. The accumulation of mail, which Butch had daily emptied from the box out front and hidden in a wood chest on the back porch, was mostly junk.

Lighting his pipe, Jay leaned back, reliving his adventures. It had been an experience, his night at the Ferry Inn. But, even now that he could afford to pay for the hospitality, he was out of his class. Acceptance by such people no longer mattered to him. He was quite content with the ordinary hominess about him. Such polish as made you hesitate to touch things, to walk across the floor even, required the vigilance of many servants or hours of personal elbow-grease, neither of which he was prepared to provide. Jay was a neat housekeeper, but not persnickety. His furniture wore the patina of grime from long, hard usage, which he had hardly noticed before. So, why disturb it? As good-natured Charley Tarbutton used to say when his overburdened wife lagged behind with her housework, "Be it ever so dirty, there's no place like home."

Their personal easy corner where he and Jack spent their leisure hours suited him perfectly. His comfortable brown wing chair, with a carpet-covered hassock, faced the padded window-seat where his pal relaxed. Beyond the triple windows a flourishing, richly green Magnolia refreshed the gaze, and in season offered gorgeous blooms. At his right elbow stood an end-table with double drawers, drop leaves and handsomely carved legs, a treasure in walnut picked up for a song at a farm sale. On it he kept his student lamp, electrified from oil, and framed photographs of all his family, not forgetting Josh and Jack. Inside its drawers he stored tobacco, extra eyeglasses, and a package of Jack's favorite sugar biscuits. On his left was a quaint trunk, vintage of Grampa Malone's youth, where among other things he treasured, Jay kept the old gentleman's big American flag and his service pistol. Above, on a wide shelf supported by ornate brackets, he kept his collection of books and the little country Gothic clock, object of barter by some unknown Malone long departed. Its busy tick-tock had the vigor of youth alongside the measured, dignified TICK-TOCK of the Ferry grandfather; and its hoarse, tinny striking sounded not unlike someone beating on a tin pan with a spoon, raucous compared with the mellow chimes of the stately aristocrat. In his cozy nook Jay was quite content. It felt good to be home.

In the early evening Jay rang Catherine Warren to let her and Butch know that he had returned. Their landlady's news chilled him. "Oh, Mr. Malone, I was waiting for your call. Mrs. Warren and the children had to leave for Iowa on a moment's notice because of a death in her family. An auto accident killed her father and left her mother hurt badly. Poor dear, she was so upset. An uncle of hers came in his car to take them and their things. She seemed to think it ain't likely she'll get back here. I have her address, if you want it. She said you'll be hearing from her. And Butch wanted me to tell you that he had arranged with the twins to care for your mail."

Jay was stunned. He could hardly speak. "How sorry I am to hear this," he managed to say. "Yes, I would like her address, thank you." He hung up and sat staring straight away. Jack watched him anxiously.

This was tragic! Having to give up her job where she was succeeding—she'd just recently had a raise. And to take Butch out of the school where he was doing so well... True, she had only a War Service appointment, just for the duration; yet the experience was good, and would undoubtedly prepare her for something better. In Iowa what had she to look forward to? Drudgery behind the counter of a country store left by her father, and the difficult care of her invalid mother.

As time passed during their brief acquaintance, Jay had observed her gradual recovery from the depression of early widowhood. Hers was a serene personality. A rare sunny smile and spoken responses that were soft, distinct and well-worded gave little hint of inner turmoil. Yet she must have suffered from doubts about raising her two fine children alone. Butch was an upstanding young lad and Aurora such a little doll. Why should the lot of this fine family be stagnation in some hick town miles from nowhere? Jay's anger flared. Yet he was powerless to change the course of events. She was gone. Her loss, and his, left him despairing. There was only Jack to console him.

Winter's blight kept them pretty much to themselves. The twins might drop by for help with their math homework or to join in a short stroll through the park. Hallie's only return was her gaudy Valentine addressed to dear Jack. Letters from Iowa were all too brief and infrequent. Catherine had her hands full. And Jay, living his monotonous routine, found little to write that might interest her.

Time passed uneventfully.

★ ★ ★

Chapter XIX

But there was a war on. And news items told of the great need for dogs in the service. Jay regularly did his bit contributing to the War Bond drives at his office, as well as diligently helping with the collection of scrap metal and rubber for the war effort. But more was needed. And as he read of the call for dogs, a horrible suspicion blighted his happiness.

Yet—No, he couldn't do it—send his spirited, intelligent, loving pal into the battlefield—he simply could not do it.

Not until he got a telephone call from one of Jack's sidewalk acquaintances who identified himself as John Hendry and asked if he might drop around for a moment. He was a clean-cut young man with a soft voice and gentle manner. Jack greeted him enthusiastically. Jay's heart sank. He knew what was coming. Their visitor was obviously uncomfortable, and Jay blessed him for that. He spoke of the desperate need for dogs. Those already in service had saved many lives. It was a matter of record that in the fifteen months since the war began, no patrols led by dogs had been fired on first or suffered casualties.

Jack would be trained as a messenger dog, with Hendry as one of his handlers. And when the war was over, he would receive an honorable discharge and be returned to Jay.

"Just think it over," Hendry said softly. "Here's my phone number."

Into the evening, while Jack dozed on the window seat, Jay agonized over his heartbreaking dilemma. How much easier to go himself. But he was no good. His best was pushing the War Bond drives. And there was no telling how many fine young men might live to come home if Jack was there. Then, when the war was over, the two of them would live happily ever after. He liked Hendry, and if it had to be, he could hardly ask for a kinder person.

Though he felt that it was sinful to postpone his decision, he knew that he must have a few more days with Jack before they were parted. A week's leave from the office gave him twenty-four hours a day to lavish on the dog all his loving attention, and to savor each moment, fixing it in his mind to sustain him later.

When he had verified Hendry's credentials, Jay thought he was ready. Twice he picked up the phone, twice he put it down. Finally he took himself in hand. It was arranged that Hendry should come for Jack on Monday morning, after Jay had left for the office. To personally hand him over would be torture he could not bear. And he needed the whole day, his mind occupied with urgent matters, before he could face his loss. But his thoughts kept shirking business, to imagine the sequence of events at home.

That Monday night was pure Hell. Pulling into his driveway he was overwhelmed by the big dark house. He couldn't go in. Delaying that awful moment, he walked over to the restaurant for his supper. A sour-faced biddy waited on him.

"Where's Millie?" he asked.

"Gone," was the laconic reply. "Quit to get married."

No pleasant chit-chat there to cheer him. Pretending to eat, he kept remembering the day he left the place and found Jack waiting outside.

Going home he dragged his feet. Reluctantly he unlocked his door and stepped inside the silent, empty house. There was no joyful welcome, nobody to care whether he came. The misery of it brought tears. Switching on his student lamp, he sank into his easy chair. Jack's presence was everywhere.

Doubts assailed Jay. Had he done the right thing? A little glimmer of hope crept in: perhaps Jack would fail his training. Then he could welcome him home in good conscience. Yet he knew the thought was unworthy. Jack was too intelligent to fail, and his nobility and courage would carry him through. Jay reminded himself that he had wanted to be a soldier. Now Jack, the better of the two of them, was fulfilling his dream. He should feel proud. But he was heartbroken. Wherever he looked, the vision of his wonderful pal haunted him. A dusting of sugar biscuit crumbs on the window seat choked him. Jack had such a sweet tooth. Only whisper "sugar biscuits," and he was all attention.

At last, emotionally drained, Jay went to bed... and had nightmares.

When the twins inquired for their canine friend, Jay struggled to keep his voice steady as he told them huskily that Jack had gone to be a soldier. "He'll be a messenger boy," he explained, "and carry letters for the men. Who knows, he may get a medal for bravery."

"Oh! How exciting!" they exclaimed in unison.

Jack's training lasted three months. Of course he passed. Brilliantly. There came a note from Hendry—they were so very proud of him.

Jay felt proud too. But his loneliness almost drove him to drink. Still, in public he put on his best face. Life must go on. The war couldn't last forever. Indeed, a Brookings authority had predicted that it would be short. Japan, the authority said, did not have the resources for a long war, so would make a desperate effort for a quick victory. Jay prayed that he was right. Whimsically he cut from the back of Hallie's Valentine a blue service star to hang in his window like those in the homes where men were overseas. It proclaimed his sacrifice, reminding him each evening when he came home to emptiness that he had one day less to wait for the war's end. He lived for that day.

In the market on Saturday, a dried-up old man ahead of Jay in line at the butcher's stall ordered half a pound of good liver. While it was being wrapped, he carefully detached precious stamps from his ration book and found in his pocket a moldy greenback.

The butcher, handing over his package, said pleasantly, "Eatin' this, you'll sure get your vitamines."

The old man shook his head. "Not me. This here's fer my cat." His face lit up. "I've got the liveliest little black beast you ever saw. She jest claws the bag to pieces when I fetch her the liver. I give it to her fer a special treat. When she's got her belly full, she curls up to sleep in my lap. She's comp'ny fer me. After I buried my wife I nearly went batty with jest four walls. I figger it's better to be meat hungry than love hungry."

And Jay, returning to his four walls, thought, "It's Hell to be love hungry."

All his hopes and prayers centered on a cease fire. Soon. SOON. He thought of little else. Jack's bed was ready with his neatly folded blanket, his food dishes remained as he had left them, the window seat nightly held Jay's vision of him.

The newspapers reported how the war was being waged with increasing ferocity overseas, and how "the exceptionally brave who lived to return were acclaimed as heroes by a nation eager to do homage to its gallant sons." But some "paid the price which glory ever exacts." And gold stars symbolizing a life lost in battle replaced the blue service stars in the windows. Coming from the store one evening, Jay passed such a house. Two elderly ladies stood conversing at the end of the walk. He caught a fragment of their conversation. "Yes," said one, "he gave his all. I say a man can't be any braver."

Hendry kept his promise to write, but not often, and always briefly. Yet his hasty jottings were reassuring—Jack and his handlers had so far safely fulfilled their missions. The dog had taken his war service in stride, Hendry wrote. He was unfazed by battle noises. Not once had he failed to accomplish his missions. And the work of the messenger dogs was desperately needed, since the walkie-talkies so often failed in foul weather. Jack and the men lived together, slept together, and if needed shared a bath in some handy stream. At one point Hendry wrote that Jack had made seven emergency messenger runs under fire when the regular lines of communication were out.

Through the pages of his atlas Jay kept track of their journeys further and further away from him, away on the other side of the world. Port Moresby, Nazdab, Kaiapit, Finshafen and other God-forsaken hellholes—places he had never even heard of before.

While a year and a half passed, and Jay suffered, Jack and his handlers accomplished wonders.

★ ★ ★

Chapter XX

In September 1944, Jay slipped from a ladder and sprained his back. Housebound for several days, he could do nothing but brood. To divert his thoughts, he went out to sit on the porch. From his old wicker rocking chair behind the screen of Heavenly Blue Morning Glories, he could observe people in the street going about their affairs.

At the moment nobody happened to be passing. Idly he watched construction progressing on the unwanted high-rise down the way. A monstrous hole had replaced the peaceful green woods, ruthlessly destroyed, where he and Jack used to take walks along the little stream. A sky-high yellow crane swung its long cable forth and back placing iron pieces beside beckoning workmen. Toilers in the deep excavation looked like ants.

A young woman, dressed in dark green from her hat down to her spike heels, clattered down the block. Small, with black hair, she recalled for Jay the girl he had met in Allies. Eons ago that seemed.

He watched two men move along the opposite sidewalk in single file, two steps apart. Other than the shabbiness of their clothing, they were exact opposites: the one ahead was big and burly, the one behind spare and stooped. The big fellow was full of life, loud-talking, gesticulating. His companion said nothing, shuffling along taking short steps, his chin tucked in, his eyes under the bill of his little gray cap bent on the ground. Suddenly he was brought up short by his gabby friend turning about and shouting, "Gimme sixty cents!" Obediently the old gent withdrew one hand from his coat and plunged it deep into his pants pocket. Talking, talking, the big man picked change from his friend's outstretched palm. Then single file they proceeded on their way and soon disappeared.

Sight of them left Jay depressed, thinking as he watched the old codger tagging along behind, "There but for a few years go I." Growing feeble and witless, he could count on probably none other than Jack's blind devotion.

Towards five o'clock—delivery was late that day—the postman appeared, stuffing mailboxes along the sidewalk. Not expecting much, but hoping for one of Hendry's terse reports, Jay strolled down and opened his box. Inside lay a single letter. It came from ARMY SERVICE FORCES, Office of the Quartermaster General. Sudden fear paralyzed him. A live bomb would have terrified him no more than that innocent-looking white envelope. But then he reminded himself, it could be good news. Jack was coming home!

Up the walk briskly he regained the privacy of his porch. With trembling hands he slit the envelope and drew out a letter two pages long:

"Dear Mr. Malone:

"It is with regret that I write to inform you of the death of JACK, the German Shepherd dog so generously donated by you for service with the armed forces."

Jay collapsed. His tears blurred the page. Furiously he crushed the cursed letter in his hands. Hope was lost; despair overwhelmed him. His wonderful Jack was gone forever.

Abruptly, fearful that his agony might be observed by some nosy neighbor, he got up and went indoors. Dropping into his easy chair, he sat staring straight away, his absent gaze fixed on the only bright spot in the room: a splash of sunshine lay on the dark carpet where shadows shifted as a breeze stirred the hemlock branches. Outside the bay window a gathering of little sparrows chirped excitedly, and nearby his Gothic clock ticked. He was unaware. Trying to collect his thoughts, he felt only his awful misery. He closed his eyes; yet he could not shut out the image of Jack there by his side.

The cursed letter waited. At last, switching on his reading lamp, he smoothed the crumpled pages across his knee and read on:

"Jack died in the Southwest Pacific Theatre after a career of outstanding achievement. He was a member of the first War Dog Tactical Unit operating in that theatre. The Unit was assembled at the War Dog Reception and Training Center, Beltsville, Md., in March 1943. It arrived at Port Moresby in July and went to a staging area for training and conditioning after several weeks aboard ship. In the latter part of August, the unit was first assigned to a Battalion of an Australian Division then operating near Nazdab, New Guinea.

"Traveling by plane, the Unit flew to Kaiapit, an airstrip near the front lines where a brigade was making ready for the advance up the Ramu Valley in the action to drive the Japanese back to Medang. As the brigade moved up the valley, the scout dogs worked with the reconnaissance patrols while the Command Post kept contact with the near elements by messenger dog. During this advance, the dogs worked out satisfactorily.

"In October, the War Dog Unit was reassigned to a Marine Raider Regiment of the Sixth Army. Again traveling by plane, the dogs and their handlers went to another staging area. In December, the Raiders moved to Finschafen to take part in the Cape Gloucester operations. The entire Dog Detachment went ashore with the first wave and figured prominently in the operation.

"Until March, the dogs were used continuously for patrol and messenger work. Lines were gradually extended to make contact with the Army Forces near Gilnit. In these weeks, there was not a single instance in which any of the dogs failed to accomplish a mission, nor was there an instance when a patrol led by a War Dog was fired upon first or suffered casualties; in contrast, dogless patrols suffered casualties, usually as a result of ambush or surprise attacks.

"During this period, the patrols led by dogs were officially credited with 180 Japanese casualties and 20 prisoners. Messenger dogs were especially useful, since the use of walkie-talkies was often impractical, due to terrific downpours and other unfavorable weather conditions.

"Jack, trained as a messenger dog, was unafraid of battle noises from the first. Throughout the period of the Cape Gloucester campaign, he distinguished himself on many occasions. His two handlers, Technicians 4th Grade William A. Matthews and John C. Hendry, reported enthusiastically on his consistently fine performance. His outstanding act of heroism was carried out during the advance on the airstrip. Near Turzi Point, the advance units were held up by Japanese pillboxes and fortifications and the aid of artillery could not be sought by the walkie-talkies, which were temporarily out of commission. A message was dispatched by Matthews back to Battalion Command Post through JACK. Although the dog had not seen Hendry since the night before, and although Hendry had changed his position and was then in a new location, JACK unerringly found his way to Hendry's foxhole. JACK had to travel through the tall Kunai grass, swim a river, and for part of the distance make his way beneath a curtain of mortar and tank fire; he finally had to jump a barbed wire fence that protected Hendry. As a result of this message, artillery fire was directed on the Japanese defenses, pulverizing them and permitting the American forward units to resume their advance."

An agony of grief convulsed Jay. As he read "curtain of mortar and tank fire," horror seared him. All shot to pieces, that's what! Goddam! Bitterly he reproached himself for deserting poor Jack. Yet even in his torment he knew that he was duty-bound. Cruelly duty-bound.

An hour of despair passed before he could bring himself to finish reading the cursed letter:

"This office has been working on a plan for the official recognition of outstanding heroism on the part of War Dogs. It is our pleasure to inform you that a citation will shortly be sent to you, awarded posthumously to JACK.

"I hope that the knowledge of JACK's remarkable record will compensate in a measure to you for his loss, and I trust that you will feel that your patriotic sacrifice has not been in vain; for there are many American boys today who owe their lives directly to the heroism of JACK, the War Dog, and indirectly to you who gave him up to serve your country."

Tears stung Jay's eyes. Try as he might, he could not console himself with pride in Jack's heroism and the many lives saved. He could only suffer. Slumped in his chair, his face stony, his thoughts filled with visions—Jack, his beloved companion, so adoring and faithful, there now in spirit only. Jack, the brave soldier, who fulfilled with unswerving devotion to duty his perilous missions through hell on earth. Over and over and over again.

Rainy dusk settled deep gloom through the house—so like their first evening together. And he could think of nothing but his tragic loss. Everything else was forgotten—dinner time, the liniment rub for his ailing back. A newspaper thudding against the front door was ignored.

As the evening wore on, the silence of his big empty house, broken only by the tick-tock of his little clock, grew ever more keenly intolerable. Memories tortured him. He closed his eyes, the pictures remained. With Jack's death died his dream of their happy reunion that had sustained him. Now he had nothing to live for. Looking ahead, he shrank from the prospect of his bleak future, the years of loneliness to come. He felt drained of strength, weak of will for the struggle. And he wondered, "Why bother?"

When the clock struck ten, he bestirred himself and laid aside the letter. In the kitchen he looked upon food with distaste. But brewing a cup of coffee, he nibbled a crust of bread and some sharp cheese. Then he swallowed a sleeping pill and fell into bed.

Next morning he rose at his usual time. Darkly overcast sky promised continued falling weather. Resolutely avoiding a glance in the direction of Jack's neat bed over in the corner, he went to the kitchen and fixed his usual breakfast of scrambled eggs, toast with marmalade, and coffee. When he had finished his usual tidying up, he showered and shaved, and dressed for the office, wearing his showiest tie and a neatly folded handkerchief peeping from his breast pocket.

Then he phoned his lawyer, Will Dawson, the roommate of his University days who had remained his good friend ever since.

"Hi, Will. How's things?"

"First rate, Jay. What's up?"

"Why, I need you to handle a little matter for me. I'm out of the office for a few days. I sprained my back. But it's about well. I wonder if you can drop by on your way home this evening?

"Sorry. Not tonight, Jay. I'm staying downtown for a meeting. But I'll be coming out around lunch time and can stop then. Say about eleven-thirty? Will that do just as well?"

"Even better. My doorbell is temporarily out of order. And since I may not hear you knock, come around the house to the bay window. It will be open and I'll be sitting just inside."

Remembering yesterday's newspaper, he tossed it into the trash. Then he disconnected the doorbell. A quick look around assured him that the house was nicely in order.

In the drawer of his little end-table he found his pen and writing paper. A glimpse of Jack's box of sugar biscuits gave him a pang. "Being of sound mind," he wrote, with a sardonic chuckle. And he wondered—Now how does the rest of it go? Oh, well, just get said what's important. "I herewith leave all my worldly possessions to Mrs. Catherine Warren and her children. This is my last will and testament, superseding any previous document on record. Signed—John Jay Malone III." To this he clipped his card with her Iowa address. And on top he left a quick note: "Sorry, Will. I have no one else to call on but you. There's room for me beside my mother up home. And you know where the money is."

From the top of his antique trunk he swept a clutter of books and papers. Raising the lid he lifted out Grampa Malone's big American flag and the old soldier's service six-shooter. With great care he draped the flag across the window seat. Against the wall he arranged treasured photographs of John Jay Malone I and John Jay II, with III and IV side by side, taken together. Underneath he placed the Quartermaster General's letter.

Settled back in his easy chair, sadly smiling at the loved ones, smoke curling upward from his pipe, he remained lost in remembrance of Jack, so unique in all his lovableness. What a wonderful character he was! So obliging in games with the rowdy kids, such a dignified companion on their quiet walks together, so incredibly intelligent and brave in performing his soldierly responsibilities. Jack's, he thought, was a shining example of an exemplary life.

In the silence of his big empty house, the Malone family clock, on its small shelf above Jay's head, loudly ticked off the minutes. There was a rasping displacement of its works, a clearing of its throat so to speak, and it began eleven resounding strokes that were like the heavy beat of a drum.

Calmly Jay lifted Grampa Malone's little Colt to his temple and put an end to his misery.

His dreams of war service had been fulfilled.

★ ★ ★

Eilleen Gardner Galer

Author/Photographer

∾

Eilleen Galer was born in Charlotte, North Carolina in 1906. She is a freelance writer and has been a photographer for over 70 years, specializing in the preservation of animals and vanishing scenes and lifestyles. She was an officer for 20 years in the National Photographic Society in Washington, DC, and received the NPS Shaw Memorial Trophy for outstanding service in 1961. Her work is in the permanent collection of the National Photographic Society of America. Ms. Galer developed and presented a humane education outreach program for the Arlington Animal Welfare League, which included a photo essay designed to promote kindness to animals. This program has been viewed by more than 10,000 people of all ages.

Eilleen Galer recently authored a biography titled *Eugen Weisz, Painter–Teacher*, and a photographic book *God Barking in Church: And Further Glimpses of Animal Welfare*, both currently in bookstores. She also has contributed to two editions of the photographic book series *American Photographers at the Turn of the Century*, also available in bookstores. She has contributed to *Cats* magazine, *Cat Fancy*, *Advocate* (American Humane Association) and the *Journal of the Photographic Society of America*. She has been a *National Finalist* in the *Washington Star* animal category, *First* for farm animals by the American Humane Association, and won the *First Place Cup* for monochrome prints and color slides and *Print of the Year* by the National Photographic Society, Washington, DC.

Eilleen Galer's sparkling wit and charming style enliven her stories enabling future generations to know, appreciate, and cherish past lifestyles and events.

Additional titles showcasing the work of Eilleen Gardner Galer:

Eugen Weisz: Painter—Teacher

God Barking in Church
And further Glimpses of Animal Welfare

The Art of the Human Form

American Photographers at the Turn of the Century
Nature & Landscapes

American Photographers at the Turn of the Century
Travel & Trekking

Just Folks - Here and There

Available from Five Corners Publications